SEP. 16. 1994

D0426754

ETHICS

ETHICS

Susan Neiburg Terkel

Lodestar Books
Dutton   New York

*This book is dedicated
to my husband,
Larry*

This book was written with support from the Charles Rieley Armington
Research Program on Values in Children.

Library of Congress Cataloging-in-Publication Data

Terkel, Susan Neiburg.
    Ethics / Susan Neiburg Terkel.—1st ed.
        p.   cm.
    Includes bibliographical references (pp. 124–126) and index.
    Summary: Examines issues of ethics, how ethics affect all aspects of our
lives, and how we determine right from wrong.
    ISBN 0-525-67371-7
    1. Ethics—Juvenile literature.   2. Teenagers—Conduct of life.
[1. Ethics.   2. Conduct of life.]   I. Title.
BJ1661.T47   1992
170—dc20   91-32006
                                                                        CIP
                                                                         AC

Published in the United States by Lodestar Books, an affiliate of Dutton
Children's Books, a division of Penguin Books USA Inc.,
375 Hudson Street, New York, New York 10014

Published simultaneously in Canada by McClelland & Stewart, Toronto

Editor: Rosemary Brosnan   Designer: Marilyn Granald, LMD

Printed in the U.S.A.   First Edition
10 9 8 7 6 5 4 3 2

ACKNOWLEDGMENTS

Gratitude goes to my editor, Rosemary Brosnan; to my agent, Andrea Brown, who first suggested I write about ethics; and especially to my advisor, Mary Mahowald, Ph.D., who so patiently helped me with this book. I would also like to thank the Charles Rieley Armington Research Program on Values in Children of Case Western Reserve University for their research grant and belief in this project.

Further thanks to the numerous people who so generously gave their time and advice: Martha E. Jones, Harold Kelvin, Harold Quigley, and Howard Radest, Ph.D., of the American Ethical Union; Reverend C. Read Heydt, John A. Bolen, Ph.D., of the National Council on Religion and Public Education; David Brooks, Ph.D., of the Thomas Jefferson Research Center; Michael Schulman, Ph.D., Young Jay Mulkay, Ph.D., of the Character Education Institute; Chuck Burlingame, Ph.D.; the Carnegie Hero Fund Commission; William Damon, Ph.D.; Jean Graznier and Ann Medlock of the Giraffe Project; Alan Gleitsman of the Gleitsman Foundation; Stuart Greenbaum of the Golden Rule Campaign; Ruth Lester of B'nai B'rith's A World of Difference; and Gordon Vars, Ph.D.

Further appreciation goes to others who so kindly offered advice and encouragement or critiqued various stages of the manuscript. These include Diana Beebe, Blanche Clegg, Pat Jenkins, Dale Marino, Bernice Massey,

Yvonne Ponsor, Michael Quigley, Tom Schneider, Athene Tarrant, Jim Wilkens, and Marilyn Wise.

My gratitude goes to the teenagers who took such a keen interest in the book, advising me about what needed clarification. These fine young readers are Eli Burstein, Debbie Crotteau, Jim Hobbes, Carrie Ludwig, Heather Niebiola, Cara Paget, Andrew Tatko, Ari Terkel, and Marni Terkel.

And finally, thank you to my husband, Larry. He was with me all the way, helping me meet every challenge by discussing each issue and listening to countless drafts and revisions.

CONTENTS

1

A RECIPE FOR LIVING

There is more to life than money, power,
fame and self-interest.

—AMITAI ETZIONI

Thirteen-year-old Brent Miller was in a motel room, searching for his father's misplaced watch. Not only did he find the missing watch, he found another lost item as well—a wallet containing five hundred dollars in cash, several credit cards, a blank check, and a driver's license. Brent called the owner of the wallet and promised to mail his wallet back to him. "It makes me feel good to be honest," he said.[1]

As it did for Brent, being honest can make many of us feel good. To appreciate the complexity of ethics, though, we have to recognize that finding five hundred dollars in cash can also "feel good"—to spend! For though we have times like Brent's when we know right from wrong and do the right thing, we also have times when we struggle with our conscience. Times when we fail to live up to moral standards. Times when we refuse to take any blame or own up to any responsibility for our mistakes. And times when we're not sure what is right or wrong.

It's natural to ask: Is Brent *really* as honest as he seemed to be? Wasn't he *ever* tempted to keep the wallet, or at least the money in it? Did he give it back to please his parents or avoid their disapproval? Was it easy to return the wallet because he didn't need the money? Or was he foolish to ignore the chance to play finders keepers?[2]

The owner of the wallet was so grateful to get it back that he rewarded Brent with two hundred dollars. But how rewarding would it have been if the owner had turned out to be a jerk who couldn't even say thank you?

Although many people are as honest as Brent, they are not necessarily honest all the time. Research about honesty shows that while most people return lost cash belonging to someone they know, only one in four returns it if the cash belongs to someone he or she doesn't know. Even fewer people return money that belongs to an institution or the government.[3] That puts Melvin Kiser, a telephone repairman, in the minority.

In Columbus, Ohio, nearly a million dollars fell out of an armored truck. Hundreds of motorists stopped their cars to gather it up. There was even a sense of camaraderie among them as one fellow shouted, "It's money . . . it's ours . . . it's ours. Grab you some while you can!"

Melvin Kiser was one of the motorists. He cheerfully gathered up fifty-seven thousand dollars. Soon, though, his cheer soured as he wrestled with his conscience over keeping the money. After two hours of moral struggle, Kiser finally decided that given his job he didn't really need the money, and that it was wrong to keep it. He turned the money in.

Afterward, Kiser's mother told him how proud she was. "That's the way I raised you," she said. But his father chastised him for being so honest. "I thought I raised you better than that," he said. Nor was his father alone. Many people agreed. For as the research on honesty indicates, most people did not return the money they found. About nine hundred thousand dollars of the one million dollars was never recovered.[4]

Returning lost objects is just one moral test. We are constantly challenged by others. Is it ever right to smoke marijuana? Copy someone else's term paper? Read your sister's diary? Break a law you think is unfair? Have premarital sex? With such decisions, the question of ethics comes into focus. Each decision deals with moral "right" and "wrong," which is what ethics is all about.

What Is Ethics?

Because ethics is about the meaning of life and the search for right from wrong, it is abstract and difficult to define. Words limit what we can convey about moral living. Like the joy of a sunlit day or the power of riding a huge wave, it must be experienced to be fully understood. Nevertheless, much has been written about ethics and added to our understanding of it.

Ethics began as unwritten rules. From the time that humans lived together in groups and established rules for the way they treated one another, people engaged in ethical inquiry. The first incidents requiring moral consideration probably led to rules about killing and about property, which determined when it was right or wrong to kill another person or for people to protect what they owned.

Although all ancient societies and religions had moral codes—rules for behavior—it was during the fifth century B.C. in Greece that the philosopher Socrates gave ethics its formal beginning. In fact, the word ethics comes from the Greek word *ethos*, which means "character."

Socrates asked his fellow Greeks to look at *why* they did what they did and thought what they thought. Questioning the meaning and value of life, he asked: What is justice? What is a good life? Can virtue be taught?

Socrates' student, Plato, and Plato's student, Aristotle, further developed Socrates' philosophy of ethics. Their thinking was so profound and complete that some philosophers comment that nothing new has been said since Plato or Aristotle. For centuries, many scholars have searched for fresh insight into the same basic questions explored by the Greek philosophers: What is the purpose of life and how can we live a good one?

The Good Life

By helping us determine what is important in life, ethics helps us set goals for what we can and ought to achieve. In devoting themselves to the attainment of human rights, for example, Abraham Lincoln, Rosa Parks (a black woman who refused to give up her seat on a bus in Montgomery, Alabama, in 1955, thereby instigating the Civil Rights movement), and Andrei Sakharov (Soviet Nobel Peace Prize winner who championed human rights in his country) all led morally good lives—full, rich, purposeful lives. So did Samantha Smith from Maine, who was only thirteen when she died in a tragic airplane crash.

In 1983, when the Soviets and Americans were still carrying on the Cold War, Samantha wrote to Soviet leader Yuri Andropov about her concern over nuclear war. When he received her letter, President Andropov invited her to visit the Soviet Union, which she did in July 1984. There she fostered a friendship between the two nations and became a national heroine of goodwill.[5]

Regardless of circumstances, setting a moral goal is available to anyone. Viktor Frankl, author of *Man's Search for Meaning*, discovered that even in the hellish confines of a concentration camp like Auschwitz, where people could no longer hold onto familiar goals, they could still choose to have a moral reason for living.[6]

Recipe for Living

Ethics guides us to the "good life" by giving us a recipe for living. This includes rules, principles, and values about how we all can and should conduct ourselves.

Thou shalt not's. Certain moral rules set limits on our behavior and provide us with a "floor of decency." By telling us what we should *not* do, they prohibit us from abusing the rights of others or causing harm. One such moral rule is: "Do not harm an innocent person." Another is: "Do not bear false witness."

Thou shalt's. From principles about what we *should* do, we acquire moral duties and learn what is expected of us, as members of families, communities, professions, and even the human race. Treat others as you would have them treat you, respect the rights of others, play fair, be loyal to your country, and give to charity. These are just a few examples of moral duties we learn in our American culture.

Beyond the call of duty. Ethics inspires us to what Mary Mahowald, a medical ethicist at the University of Chicago, calls virtue, or *moral excellence.* "Virtue," Mahowald suggests, "means going beyond what we are obliged to do."[7]

For example, we have no duty, either legal or moral, to donate our bone marrow, kidneys, or blood to anyone, not even a close relative. Nor do we have a duty to send money to flood victims or even help the elderly across a street. That we do, however, is a virtue—"beyond the call of duty."

In All the Right Places

Morality is not a "thing apart," a separate area of life.[8] It is a part of everything, from our personal lives to public affairs and global concerns.

At home and school, it helps us decide how to treat our family and friends. At work, it helps us decide how honestly and how earnestly to perform our jobs, and even what kind of professions we choose. It shapes our public agenda and the way we treat members of our society. It raises hundreds of important questions: Does random drug testing infringe on the right to privacy? Is it right to enter into a legal agreement to be a surrogate parent or to renege on such an arrangement? Should a journalist be required to reveal his or her sources? Should our nation help defend a nation that disregards basic human rights?

Ethics is not separate from politics, economics, art, religion, or other aspects of our lives. The same moral issue can appear in many areas. For example, several states, including Wisconsin, Connecticut, New York, and Illinois, have laws forbidding married persons to have sex with anyone other than their spouses.[9] Although no one in Wisconsin could recall the last time the law had been enforced, in 1990, Donna E. Carroll was prosecuted there for committing adultery. She faced up to a two-year prison sentence and a ten-thousand-dollar fine.

For Donna Carroll, adultery is private and therefore a personal moral decision. For the attorney prosecuting her, it was a matter of professional ethics to prosecute the case. For the lawmakers who continue to uphold that law, it was an issue of protecting the family. And for many others, it was a question of privacy: Does government have the right to legislate morality?

Because ethics is so broad and complex, it is easier to understand if we divide it into smaller, though overlapping, subjects. Following is a brief sample of ethical subjects.

Personal ethics. Personal ethics involves our character and the kind of person we are. It is the process of making ethical judgments and decisions. Through the moral values, rules, and principles we acquire, the standards we strive to keep, and the goals we try to reach, we develop a code that determines how we think and act morally. Should I go to the movies or visit my grandmother? Is lying ever right? Do I still have a duty to help others even when I may be in danger?

Religious ethics. For thousands of years, religions have been a major source of moral ideals and values. Many of their teachings have filtered into our communities, schools, and laws.

Although the world's religions offer many different viewpoints on how to live a good life, they also share very basic views about moral truth. Perhaps one of the most important is how to treat one another. Five hundred years before Jesus preached the Golden Rule: "Do unto others as you would have them do unto you," Confucius taught his Chinese followers a similar moral rule: "Do not do unto others what you would not they should do unto you."[10]

And Red Jacket, a Native American, said, "We have our religion. It teaches us to be thankful for all the favors we receive; to love each other, and to be united."[11]

Legal ethics. On issues such as human rights, gun control, capital punishment, and abortion, ethics and law converge—and often conflict.

In court, victims of moral wrongdoing can find redress and restitution. Medical ethical dilemmas are often settled in court. The world court addresses crimes against humanity. In these various ways, laws dictate many personal moral principles.

Medical ethics. The field of medicine raises some of our thorniest ethical issues. Should the life-support systems of patients who are dying or are irreversibly unconscious be removed? Do parents with certain religious beliefs have the right to refuse medical treatment for their children if that treatment runs counter to their religious teachings? Is it ever fair to withhold medical information from patients, or to disclose information to others without the patient's consent? Is it right to begin human lives in a laboratory, rather than in women's bodies, or to use human subjects for medical research? When enough medical resources are not available for all who need them, who should get them?

Professional ethics. Ethics is an important aspect of the work we do. The "work ethic" that guides our society—be productive and succeed—sets a standard for how we work and the kind of work we choose to do.

The main purpose of professional ethics, though,

is to ensure that the members of a profession live up to that profession's ethical standards. When physicians take the Hippocratic oath, for example, they promise to uphold their profession's ethic for helping the sick and injured.

Journalists are expected to follow their profession's ethical standard by reporting the truth. The American Bar Association sets ethical standards for lawyers to uphold the legal profession. Government officials are expected to honor the public's trust in them.

To ensure that its members act in an ethical manner, many professions have ethical codes and ethics committees. The committees may even have the power to expel members who are found guilty of ethical wrongdoing. For example, both the Senate and the House of Representatives have ethics committees. In 1990, the Senate Ethics Committee investigated seven senators—a record number—for questionable financial dealings.[12]

By helping us make wise decisions, add purpose to our lives, and teach us to be fair and kind, ethics deepens our understanding of ourselves and the world we live in. It also provides a challenge to the way we think and act.

2

IN ALL THE RIGHT PLACES

When Tami Norton swam with dolphins in Florida as part of a study program, she became quite attached to them. "There were no words," she explained, "but you could feel a friendship."[1] Then Tami learned that in the last three decades as many as ten million dolphins had died in the nets of tuna fishermen even though there were safer ways to fish for tuna.[2]

Morally committed to saving dolphins from fishing nets, Tami and a few other students who had gone on the trip with her organized a tuna boycott in their high school in Aurora, Colorado; they convinced their school to eliminate tuna from its lunch menu. Similar pressure from around the country prodded three major U.S. tuna distributors to switch to dolphin-safe fishing methods.

Until Tami and others like her learned of the threat to dolphins, eating tuna fish (or choosing not to eat it) had been a rather routine decision, a question of taste and nutrition, not morals. But as they grew aware and concerned, whether or not to eat tuna became a moral issue.

In his book, *Diet for a New America*, vegetarian guru John Robbins advocates practical health reasons for becoming vegetarian, such as lowering cholesterol levels and avoiding the residual antibiotics found in meat. Since these reasons have nothing to do with whether it is right or wrong to kill living beings for food, they are amoral, or morally neutral reasons for not eating meat. (Both terms, *amoral* and *morally neutral*, refer to situations that are neither moral nor immoral.)

However, when Robbins advises readers not to eat "anything that has [a] face . . . sexual urges . . . a mother or father . . . or tries to run away from you,"[3] he is treating the issue *morally*, and claiming that it is *wrong* to eat certain animal foods.

Avoiding harm to animals is not the only moral reason for a vegetarian diet. In her book, *Diet for a Small Planet*, Frances Moore Lappé discusses political and environmental reasons as well. Raising cattle consumes a great deal of water, mostly expended for irrigating the crops that feed the livestock. In fact, as much water as an average family uses in a week goes into producing a quarter-pound hamburger.[4] Furthermore, beef uses fifteen times more water than it takes to produce vegetable protein.[5] In order to conserve both water and grazing land, and produce enough food to feed everyone in the world, Lappé advocates a moral commitment to a vegetarian diet.

For most nonvegetarians, eating meat, tuna, and even lobsters boiled alive is not a moral issue at all. They argue that it is a natural "law of the jungle," neither right nor wrong, and a simple part of the food chain.

Suggesting that what you eat can be a moral issue is not intended to make you a vegetarian! Rather, it is to illustrate a key ingredient of ethics, which is *moral awareness*—being aware that a situation may be an ethical one for some people and not for others.

Tuning In

You are already aware of the *moral dimension* of many situations. Parents, teachers, and religious leaders often create this awareness. Public education also helps us become more attuned to moral issues. Through a barrage of publicity, for instance, organizers of Earth Day 1990 brought moral awareness to ecological issues like pollution, deforestation, and depletion of the ozone layer.

Sometimes it is through fear and ignorance that moral awareness is raised. Before scientists discovered how AIDS was transmitted, many people acquired it from blood transfusions tainted by the virus. This is how thirteen-year-old Ryan White had contracted AIDS.[6]

Out of fear and ignorance that their children would get AIDS from Ryan, many parents protested his attendance at school. As a result, school officials in his hometown of Kokomo, Indiana, barred Ryan from attending classes.

Since Ryan knew his classmates couldn't get AIDS from casual contact with him, he felt he had a moral (and legal) right to attend school. With national publicity focused on his case, Ryan challenged the school board and won. (In hopes of finding greater tolerance elsewhere, however, his family moved to nearby Cicero, Indiana, where Ryan was not only allowed to attend school but was warmly welcomed.)

In the next five years, before dying of AIDS at the age of eighteen, Ryan became a beloved national hero. He raised the public's moral consciousness about AIDS and widespread discrimination against AIDS patients.

Reaching for the Brass Ring

Tuning in to moral awareness is only part of the moral recipe. Two other key ingredients are *moral standards* to reach for and *moral goals* to achieve. Both require a moral *imagination*—an ability to picture the kind of person you strive to be and the sort of world in which you strive to live.[7]

Moral standards define the best we can be and the most moral way we can behave.

Through her high moral standards, Rosemary Pritchett, a homeless mother of three, met Cheryl Wood, a nurse from Kansas City, Missouri. And because Cheryl Wood had high moral standards, Ms.

Pritchett and her three children now live in a fine home.[8]

On the day that Rosemary Pritchett withdrew all twelve hundred dollars she had saved from Social Security disability payments to bid on a run-down, abandoned house, she found a check for four hundred dollars lying on the street. On the check was an address and a name—Cheryl Wood, who had also endorsed the back of the check.

"I know unscrupulous people could have got it cashed," said Ms. Pritchett. "But that thought never crossed my mind."

After thumbing through several pages of Woods in the telephone book, she found the one whose address matched that on the check, and called Cheryl Wood to tell her where she could retrieve it.

Mrs. Wood came to the shelter for the homeless, where the Pritchetts were living until they could move into their house, and met Ms. Pritchett. They became friends.

When Ms. Pritchett moved into the dilapidated house she had purchased from the county, Mrs. Wood came to visit her. She saw that the house had crumbling walls, that vandals had ripped out the wiring and plumbing, that sewer pipes had frozen and burst, and that the foundation was weak. So, ignoring her lawyer husband's advice not to set her standards too high, she called contractors, suppliers, and craftspeople, who generously volunteered labor and materials.

The contractor supervised the renovation; an

electrical company rewired the house; a plumber installed a water heater; a supplier built windows and provided other materials that a retired maintenance engineer installed—all for free. After the media reported the new friendship resulting from the lost check, even more help poured in.

Not everyone has a positive moral imagination. Sometimes, where people live and how they are treated is so awful they have difficulty knowing right from wrong or believing that their world can improve.

In contrast, eleven-year-old Trevor Ferrell had a moral imagination that set high goals, envisioning a world where the homeless would be cared for. Unlike Mrs. Wood, however, Trevor did not wait until he was faced with an opportunity to help. He went out looking for one.[9]

Trevor lived in a lovely suburb of Philadelphia, far removed from the homeless in his city. After hearing about their plight on the news, he became so curious and concerned that one night his parents drove him into the city to meet some homeless people. Before leaving, Trevor grabbed his blanket and special pillow to give to a needy person.

As the Ferrells headed into downtown Philadelphia, Trevor held the blanket under the car heater to warm it up. Soon they saw a shoeless man lying on a street grate. While his father stood near him, Trevor approached the stranger and offered him his blanket. The homeless man was surprised at first, but then he burst into a smile, thanking Trevor for his kindness.

Trevor felt so good that he returned the next night, this time with two more blankets. In fact, night after night the Ferrells returned. Their station wagon soon became a familiar sight. They brought sandwiches, soup, and coffee, and, in time, they knew many of the homeless people by name.

One night Trevor found a letter tucked in the windshield of his family's car. "Last night in my loneliness, poverty, and utter despair I could have ended it all. It was freezing cold and pouring rain . . . Suddenly in front of me stood a little boy with a face of spring, who gave me a respectful 'Here, sir, I have a blanket for you.' He had given me more than a blanket; he gave me a new hope. I could not keep back the tears. I fell in love with that little boy named Trevor, and at the same time I fell in love again with life."

When the Ferrells ran out of spare clothing and blankets, Trevor asked people in his church and at his father's hardware store for donations for the homeless. The local newspaper wrote about Trevor's campaign.

Soon Trevor's vision of a better city spread to others as dozens volunteered their time, food, clothing, and even a roomy house.

When some of Trevor's classmates taunted him about his campaign and all the attention he was getting, he took them on a nightly food run. By night's end, Trevor had three new volunteers.

In time, Trevor's Place, a shelter where the homeless could sleep and look for jobs, opened. After that
came a thrift store to raise money for the project,
then Next Door, a residence and training center for
single mothers and their children. Because of Trevor's moral imagination, by 1991 his organization
was serving more than two hundred people a day,
and fifteen cities across America had set up
branches.[10]

The Good Life

By raising our moral consciousness and setting
moral standards and goals—to be a good person, live
a morally good life, and make the world better—we
embrace ethical values.

Living a morally good life depends largely on what
you start, not what you finish, what you strive for,
not what you reach. Most of all, it depends on the
kind of person you aspire to be and the kind of world
you imagine to be possible. And with such striving
comes success.

Perhaps one of the best definitions of success is
attributed to nineteenth-century philosopher Ralph
Waldo Emerson: Success is "to leave the world a
better place, whether by a healthy child, a garden
patch, or a redeemed social condition; to know even
one life has breathed easier because you have lived."

It is not always possible to wake people up to
moral issues. Nor do the moral standards of people
like Tami Norton, Ryan White, Rosemary Pritchett,

Cheryl Wood, Trevor Ferrell, and others transform themselves or the world into moral perfection.

Still, sparked by awareness and guided by imagination, such people act on their moral convictions. As their actions ripple and spread, they spur hope in us all.

3

FOR GOODNESS' SAKE

Everybody can be great because anybody can serve [the Civil Rights movement]. You don't have to have a college degree to serve, you don't have to make your subject and verb agree to serve, you don't have to know about Plato and Aristotle to serve, you don't have to know Einstein's 'Theory of Relativity' to serve, you don't have to know the Second Theory of Thermodynamics and Physics to serve.

You only need a heart full of grace, a soul generated by love.

—MARTIN LUTHER KING, JR.[1]

As fifteen-year-old Gary Lawrence walked through his trailer park on his way home, he saw flames shooting through the windows of a neighbor's trailer.

Knowing that the neighbor was an elderly, blind man, Gary rushed over, broke down the front door, and boldly entered. Once inside, he seized a fire extinguisher and immediately tried to put out the flames. As Gary struggled with the fire, which was already out of control, he heard the old man yelling for help.

Gary dashed into the hall, grabbed the man, and dragged him to the back door. Finding the back steps broken, he hopped down and convinced the man to jump, then caught him and dragged him through the smoke-filled yard to safety.

Within seconds of Gary's rescue, the trailer collapsed in flames.

Having grown up with fire fighters, Gary knew how to deal with fires. Still, to save his neighbor, he had to risk his own life. Was Gary attracted to adventure, to the danger of such a rescue? Was he trying to be a hero? Or was he simply motivated by the "goodness of his heart"?

"It was like a second instinct," Gary explained.[2]

In a less dramatic, but no less moral spirit, Edith Imre gives away more than a thousand high-quality wigs a year to burn victims, cancer patients, and people who have gone bald for a variety of reasons and who can't afford to buy a wig. Some of the wigs are worth as much as fifteen thousand dollars. "Ten psychiatrists can't do as much good as you can by putting a wig on the head of a woman with cancer," Mrs. Imre says. "The most devastating thing is to be bald."[3]

What motivates Edith Imre to give so generously? Does she do it for publicity or tax breaks, or simply to feel good about herself? Is she a naturally good person or did an experience in her life teach her generosity?

It doesn't take much more than watching the evening news to be cynical about human nature, and wonder where the good side is much of the time. Or to question the motives of the good deeds we do hear about.

Based on his professional experience, Sigmund Freud, pioneer of modern psychiatry, concluded that people are fundamentally selfish and aggressive, and have no natural inclination toward kindness or justice.[4]

Other philosophers such as Aristotle, John Locke, and Jean-Jacques Rousseau believed that we are born mentally and emotionally "blank"—tabula rasa— and therefore, to be ethical we must be taught or trained in moral behavior.

Then there are the optimists who claim that humans are born with naturally kind and good temperaments, albeit to varying degrees.[5]

If we are selfish and aggressive, as Freud suggested, can we learn to be good? If we are born a blank slate, how do we acquire moral training or improve our moral development? And what can we do for those who are short-changed in natural goodness?

Growing Up Moral

Jean Piaget, a French psychologist, closely observed children to find out what they think about right and wrong. From his observations, he concluded that children go through well-defined stages of moral development and that during the early stages we shouldn't expect them to reason or behave as well as adults.[6]

In the 1970s, Lawrence Kohlberg, of Harvard University, expanded Piaget's theory. To measure their moral reasoning, Kohlberg asked boys to discuss their reactions to hypothetical moral dilemmas. By studying their responses, he concluded that just as they grow physically in stages, they also pass through six stages of moral reasoning.

The Heinz Dilemma

In Europe, a woman was near death from cancer. There was one drug that the doctors thought might save her— a form of radium that a druggist in her town had recently discovered. The drug was expensive to make, but the druggist was charging ten times what the drug cost him to produce. He paid $200 for the radium and charged $2000 for a small dose of the drug.

The sick woman's husband, Heinz, went to everyone he knew to borrow the money, but he could get together only about $1000, which was half of what it cost. He told the druggist that his wife was dying and asked him to sell it cheaper or let him pay later.

But the druggist said, "No, I discovered the drug and I'm going to make money from it."

Heinz got desperate and broke into the man's store to steal the drug for his wife.[7]

Should the husband have done that? Was it right or wrong?

In the earlier stages of moral reasoning, the boys based their moral decisions on reward or punishment. "The pharmacist is overcharging for the drug; he deserves to be robbed," or "Without the drug, the wife will die; she deserves to get it, even if it means stealing" are typical responses.

In later stages, they judge what is morally right and wrong by how it conforms to others' expectations, and by what is lawful. "If you let people think they can get away with stealing, then nobody will respect the law forbidding it."

According to Kohlberg, in the most advanced stages, people use their own conscience and a sophisticated sense of justice and fairness to determine what is right or wrong. (Because Kohlberg's theory of moral development is not easy to condense, these stages have been grossly oversimplified.)[8]

Research by Carol Gilligan, a professor at Harvard and Kohlberg's former student, challenges many of his conclusions, especially his definition of the highest stage of moral reasoning. For, she concludes that there is a different, equally advanced stage, where moral decisions are based on care and concern for others. "If Heinz is convicted and jailed," for example, "how will he be able to help his wife in the future?" "Why can't someone try to reason with the pharmacist and persuade him to be more humanitarian toward the wife?"

Kohlberg focused his research on moral reasoning, concluding that the highest stage is reached only after age twenty, and only by a select few.[9] Yet despite a lack of sophisticated moral reasoning, children can have rich moral values and behavior at any age.

Ten-year-old Erica Hansen, from Flagstaff, Arizona, collected and recycled bottles, walked dogs, and did other chores to raise twenty dollars a month to support a foster child through the Save the Children organization,[10] money she could easily have spent on herself. And nine-year-old Teddy Andrews started the Wish List, a list of the needs of groups and agencies that helped children, which led the way for getting donations from local businesses to make the wishes come true.[11]

Furthermore, recent studies confirm that the roots of such moral behavior—kindness and fairness—are found early in childhood.[12]

Thy Brother's Keeper

Poet Sara Teasdale wrote about a "heart that never hardens." By this she meant people who care about others, can take their point of view, and can identify with them as well; this identification is called empathy.

Empathy means sharing the feelings of other people. When they feel sad, you feel their sadness. Likewise, when they feel joy and excitement, you feel these emotions with them.

Newborns may even have the capacity to connect and empathize with others. When they hear another infant crying, many infants cry too.[13] And by ten to fourteen months, when faced with a person who is in distress, many babies empathize by whimpering or bursting into tears.[14] Martin Hoffman called this empathic response "global empathy."[15]

Of course, not all infants empathize when they see or hear someone else in pain. Some show only curiosity at someone's pain, while others even find it amusing.[16]

Within a few years, however, most toddlers can empathize, and have even learned to help a person who is in sorrow or pain. For example, seeing people in distress, they will often comfort them by offering a favorite toy or gently patting their knees.[17]

By ten to twelve years of age, children have begun to empathize with people they don't know.[18] Just hearing about someone else's plight—poverty, sickness, or other hardships—triggers empathy and feelings of what it must be like to "walk in their shoes." Likewise, hearing of the success of those far removed, such as sports heroes or rock stars, can also elicit empathy.

Researchers Miho Toi and C. Daniel Batson established that feeling empathy for someone in trouble induces a strong urge to help.[19] The more we feel for others, especially for their pain, the more likely we are to take responsibility for them, and act altruistically toward them—that is, on their behalf without expecting anything in return.

This link between empathy and altruism is found in many kind or charitable acts. "To give is to receive" refers to the satisfaction and empathy we feel from helping another person.

In December 1987, Ken Barton was stricken with aplastic anemia.[20] Without a bone marrow transplant, Ken had no chance of surviving the year. His doctors tested his mother, father, sister, and two half brothers, but no one matched Ken's tissue type.

As a result, on New Year's Eve Ken was put on a drug that had a 30 percent success rate. The drug failed. In fact, the catheter in his chest used to administer the drug gave Ken a potentially fatal infection.

While Ken was fighting the infection, his doctor put in a search request for a donor through the National Marrow Donor Program. Ken's odds were one in twenty thousand of finding a match among strangers. And time was slipping away.

With nothing to gain except the satisfaction of saving a life, hundreds of people, all of them strangers, volunteer for a blood test that can match them to someone in need of a marrow transplant. If their tissue is compatible, they enter the hospital, receive a general anesthetic, and donate their bone marrow.

On April 12, 1988, a forty-one-year-old school-teacher from Seattle donated her bone marrow to Ken. On May 25, 1988, Ken walked out of the hospital for the first time in nearly five months. Said the schoolteacher who donated the marrow: "Being able to save Ken's life was like winning the lottery."[21] It was also altruism.

Altruism might also have prompted twenty-two year-old Hat Chi Do to jump into the turbulent water below a dam in order to rescue his friend, Tu V. Huynh, who had fallen in while fishing. Although Huynh was later rescued by boaters, in the turbulence Do floundered and drowned.[22]

A Balancing Act

The classic image of the moral person is someone who detaches himself or herself from the situation in order to view it objectively and then decide, based on moral principles and rules, what is right. Lawrence Kohlberg's theory of the most advanced stage of moral reasoning included only this rational perspective on justice and fairness.

Carol Gilligan offers a "different voice," as she calls her alternative image of the moral person—a caring, compassionate person who makes a decision by determining how her behavior affects other people, especially the people she cares about. And British novelist and philosopher Iris Murdoch suggests that love for other people is the central fact of our everyday lives and morality.[23]

To illustrate these differences, consider a decision about whether or not it is wrong to cheat on a final exam. The purely rational agents will coolly detach themselves from the situation. Their sense of justice draws them to conclude that cheating is wrong because it is unfair to have an advantage over classmates who aren't cheating.

Out of self-interest or practicality, the pragmatists reason that cheating is wrong because it denies students the satisfaction of knowing they did well on their own. Or they may decide that getting a poor, but honest, grade is safer than getting punished, or losing their teacher's respect if they are caught cheating.

In contrast, Gilligan suggests that others, particularly females, based their decisions on *why* a student is compelled to cheat, and not necessarily on the "rule" about honesty they have been taught. For example, a student who is working hard to contribute money to a financially strained household and has no time to study for such an important exam might have a good reason to cheat. They also consider the alternative of discussing the situation with the teacher, and asking to take the test when they can find the time. Or, finally, they may regard cheating as wrong because it *hurts* people—the students who study and honestly take the exam, as well as the teacher who will not be able to get an accurate assessment of his or her teaching.

Human behavior is complex, and moral goodness is no exception. Perhaps a potpourri of principles will serve us best—justice and fairness, empathy and kindness, and the pride and self-respect we feel when we have done our duty or gone beyond it.

Following the teaching of Jesus, Martin Luther

King, Jr., advised us to "combine the toughness of the serpent and the softness of the dove, to have a tough mind and a tender heart."[24] To make rational decisions, we do need astute minds. But as Thomas Likuna, one of Lawrence Kohlberg's colleagues said, "We can reach high levels of moral reasoning and still behave like scoundrels."[25]

For justice without love is merely a set of principles—the letter, not the spirit, of the law. And judging from the abundance of well-intentioned misdeeds, a heart without rules to follow is dangerous. A tough mind and a tender heart—why not aspire for both?

4

LEARNING RIGHT FROM WRONG

On a cool spring evening in Central Park, a gang of boys beat, raped, and nearly murdered a young jogger who was exercising after working all day as a stockbroker.[1]

The incident evoked a harsh public outcry. It also raised many moral concerns. Why hadn't these boys learned moral restraint? Why did their parents, the schools, and society in general fail to give them character? What had arrested their moral development?

To understand the need for a strong moral education, we do not have to look at such a hideous crime. Why did the *Dartmouth Review*, a conservative weekly newspaper at a prestigious university, sponsor a free lobster-and-champagne feast to coincide with a campus fast for world hunger, publish a list of members of the school's Gay Students' Association, or run a column in "black English" suggesting that black students were illiterate?[2]

Why do 90 percent of us regularly lie?[3]

Why have seventy million Americans—nearly a third of our population—used illegal drugs?[4]

Why do affluent youngsters knock over mailboxes, vandalize school property, and make cruel racial slurs?

On the bright side, many children are learning their moral lessons. Justin Lebo spends all his allowance and all of his spare time refurbishing bikes for kids who can't afford their own. Fourteen-year-old Michael Guarrine devotes practically all of his free time to environmental work. And teenager Marcey Perry reaches out to other victims of sexual abuse with a stage presentation about her own painful experience.[5]

Morality is about how we live, so we learn it over our entire lifetime. However, during childhood and adolescence we acquire most of our moral values.

We learn right from wrong in many places. The traditional and most influential ones are the home and family, religious institutions, and school.

There's No Place Like Home

There's no place like home for early moral training. When Barbara Dafoe Whitehead, a research associate at the Institute for American Values, asked parents what their basic responsibility was, most stressed, "Teaching my kids right from wrong."[6] As other research proves, parents are one of the most important moral teachers.[7]

To learn moral responsibility, it helps if children

have warm, loving, accepting parents, as well as moral guidelines and limits. It also helps to have parents who can accept that their children, especially their teenagers, may have different moral viewpoints from their own.

Children learn from what they hear and what they see. Therefore, parents who set good moral examples themselves teach the most effective moral lessons.

In 1983, Samuel and Pearl Oliner, professors at Humboldt State University in California, conducted a study to find out what shaped the moral heroism of people who rescued others at great risk to themselves during the Holocaust.[8] Among other findings, the Oliners discovered that parents who set a good example, and who teach their children to be responsible toward all people, not simply those of their own ethnic group, are the most successful at raising morally conscious children.

In contrast, in homes where prejudice, racism, sexism, and the like prevail, parents teach their children that only "their group" counts and that anyone else doesn't matter. Children growing up in these homes have to learn their moral lessons elsewhere—and often they don't learn them at all.

In many homes, "do as I say, not as I do" is the rule. For example, parents who cheat on their company expense account, defy traffic laws, and lie about their child's age in order to get airline or theater discounts send confusing moral messages about honesty.

Even in homes where parents are good moral

teachers, children can fail to get the message—or choose to ignore it. According to a 1989 Girl Scout survey of young people, 92 percent said their parents care about them, but only 65 percent would turn to a parent for moral advice. And at least 40 percent say they prefer the advice of their friends over that of their parents.[9]

Aristotle stressed that in order to grow into a moral adult, a child needs to be trained into the habit of doing the right thing. To raise an honest child, for example, he advised praising good behavior such as telling the truth and punishing bad behavior such as fibbing.[10]

"Spare the rod and spoil the child" misleads many parents into believing that spanking, beating, verbal abuse, or withdrawal of love can "shape" their children's behavior for the better. Dispelling this myth in her book, *For Your Own Good*, Alice Miller explains that "when parents are *always* right, children learn that there is no need to rack their own brains to determine right from wrong."[11] As a result, these children never learn one of the most important ingredients in morality—to make wise choices and follow their own conscience.

Because the experiences of your childhood contribute so much to your moral values, it is easy to blame your misbehavior on parents and other caretakers. Living a truly moral life, however, means taking responsibility for yourself.

Through therapy, religion, schooling, or self-awareness, a person can break the chain of abuse, neglect, and even permissiveness. As victims of childhood trauma mourn the loss of how childhood *should* or *could* have been, they rediscover what it means to be truly themselves again—with the right to have their own moral opinions and feelings and, most of all, to follow their own conscience.

In God We Trust

Religion can give people spiritual guidance and strength, as well as a healthy perspective on morality. Belief in the divine has inspired people and nations to blaze trails of human rights, charity, and righteous living. Others find in their religion quiet strength and inspiration for their daily lives.

In her book *Ethics in America: Source Reader*, ethicist Lisa Newton points out that the "life of obedience and devotion taught in the Bible is practiced or attempted to be practiced by thousands of people."[12] In the United States alone, 43 million people attend church or synagogue.[13] And in a recent survey of young people, while only 3 percent said they turn to clergy for help with a moral problem, 82 percent said they believe in God and 40 percent pray daily.[14]

All religions have moral codes that teach their followers ethics and moral living. Through their literature, myths, and laws, they offer a wealth of ethical directives and moral teachings. In fact, biblical tradition in ethics is the oldest that we deal with, and certainly the most familiar.

Like many other world religions, Jewish Law and Christian Ways are models of ethical behavior. One of the most well-known biblical moral prescriptions is found in the Ten Commandments, in Exodus:

> I am the Lord your God. . . .
> You shall have no other gods before me.
> You shall not take the name of the Lord
>   your God in vain.
> Remember the sabbath day, to keep
>   it holy.
> Honor your father and your mother.
> You shall not kill.
> You shall not commit adultery.
> You shall not steal.
> You shall not bear false witness against
>   your neighbor.
> You shall not covet [anything that is your
>   neighbor's].

Besides the Judeo-Christian tradition, a rich diversity of world religions also teach ethics and moral behavior.

Not everyone agrees that religions inspire moral behavior. Karl Marx, the father of communism, was so critical of the influence of religion that he referred to it as the "opiate of the masses." And Sigmund Freud, the father of modern psychology, regarded organized religion as institutional "wish-fulfillment"—based on the need that people have for self-deception.[15]

In 1978, the Reverend Jim Jones, leader of the People's Temple in San Francisco, California, convinced more than nine hundred followers to resettle in his religious community deep in the jungle of Guyana, in South America.[16]

By starving, punishing, and scaring members, he coerced them into submission. Few escaped his tyranny or charismatic rule. Tragically, after Congressman Leo Ryan and several reporters flew to Guyana to investigate the commune, Reverend Jones convinced his entire religious community to commit mass suicide by ingesting soft drinks laced with cyanide.

Few religious cults are as terrible as the People's Temple. And Marx and Freud both might be judging the impact of religion too harshly. Still, there is always the risk that misguided religious beliefs—or leaders espousing them—rob members of moral agency—and sometimes moral decency.

Many people learn morality without entering a house of worship or joining an organized religion. Like Henry Thoreau, author of *Walden*, or Peace Pilgrim, a woman who spent the last twenty-eight years of her life walking for peace, people find moral guidance through meditation, inspirational reading, music, and similar pursuits.

Others, such as philosophers Jean-Paul Sartre and Friedrich Nietzsche, believed that since we have rational, creative minds, we define our own morality through our own decisions, and do not need to believe in God in order to be ethical.

One organization that believes you can be ethical without believing in God is the American Ethical Union. It was founded by Felix Adler, who had studied to be a rabbi. Adler taught the importance of sexual purity, social action, and the study of ethics.

Like other religious organizations, the American Ethical Union has weekly services and Sunday schools, performs weddings and funerals, and is involved in a number of service and social-action projects.[17]

In the Little Red Schoolhouse

In addition to the family and religion, schools teach moral education. As Kevin Ryan, professor of education at Boston University said, "School is not simply to make children smart, but to make them smart *and* good."[18]

Prior to this century, nearly all juvenile literature contained a moral lesson. Widely used stories included *McGuffey's Eclectic Readers*, Horatio Alger stories of success through hard work, and fairy tales such as those of the brothers Grimm and Hans Christian Andersen.[19] Among the most popular collection of tales was *Aesop's Fables*, written by a quick-witted servant who lived in Asia Minor during the sixth or seventh century B.C.

Legends, myths, folklore, and proverbs also instilled in students moral values and principles. For example, the well-known myth about George Washington chopping down the cherry tree taught the value of honesty, while the legend of Johnny Appleseed planting apple trees taught the value of using the gifts of nature to make the world a better place.

Benjamin Franklin, author of *Poor Richard's Almanack*, offered much common sense and wisdom with proverbs like "he that lieth down with dogs shall rise up with fleas" and "well done is better than well said."[20] His proverbs became part of our nation's moral heritage.

Historically, religion and school converged to teach morals. For nearly two centuries of public education, this right to teach morality through prayer and religious instruction went unchallenged.

The typical school day began with recitation of the Lord's Prayer and a short passage from the Bible. Posting the Ten Commandments on the classroom bulletin board further reminded students of moral lessons.

During the 1930s and 1940s, students had what was called "release time"—time apart from their regular studies. This usually amounted to a half hour or hour a week, when students were excused to attend a religious class taught by someone from one of the local churches. Most students participated in the class, but those who didn't were excused to attend study hall or go to the library.

Then in 1948, Vashti McCollum, the mother of Terry McCollum, a fifth grader who was the only student in her class to be excused from release time, sued the school board.

In an unexpected and nearly unanimous decision, the Supreme Court sided with the McCollums, striking down release time as unconstitutional and an infringement of First Amendment rights.[21] Students could no longer attend religious classes on public school grounds.

Four years later, in another case, *Zorach* v. *Clau-*

sen, the Court upheld the right to be excused from class for religious instruction if class were held elsewhere, off school grounds.[22]

Several cases that followed further eroded the school's right to teach morals through religion. First, *Engle* v. *Vitale* (1962) struck down nondenominational school prayer.[23] The Court said: "It is no part of the business of government to compose official prayers for any group of American people to recite." Then a year later, two more cases—*Abington School District* v. *Schempp* and *Murray* v. *Curlett* (1963) struck down religious school prayer as well.[24] And, in 1981, the Supreme Court struck down a Kentucky law that compelled every school to post the Ten Commandments.[25]

Despite these Supreme Court rulings against bringing religion into the public schools, the tide is changing. Opinion polls show that the majority—68 percent—of the public favors devotional school prayer.[26]

While prayer in public school continues to be struck down as unconstitutional, California, Texas, and a few other states have reintroduced religion into the public-school curriculum.

As long as a school's approach is academic, not devotional; as long as it strives for awareness of religions, not acceptance of any one religion; as long as it sponsors the study of religion, not the practice of it; and, finally, as long as it exposes students to a diversity of religious views and refrains from imposing any particular view, the study of religion is not only legal, it is meritorious.[27]

Neither religious arrogance nor religious practice belongs in public school. But failure to discuss religion at all gives students the false impression that the religious life of humankind is insignificant or unimportant.[28] For example, in 1988 New Jersey's governor, Thomas Kean, appointed experts to an advisory council that was to make suggestions for how character education could become part of the school curriculum. In their report to the governor, the council recommended teaching such desirable values as civic responsibility, patriotism, justice, honesty, courtesy, loyalty, moderation, thrift, tolerance, accountability, courage, and diligence.[29]

Schools at all levels—from elementary to university—recognize the importance of ethics, and have resumed teaching it. In some schools, ethics is taught as a separate subject. Moral lessons are abundant in subjects such as literature, social studies, and health. In science class, they are raised in regard to such issues as ecology and environmental protection, while foreign language classes offer a convenient platform for teaching about tolerance and open-mindedness.

Other schools teach ethics as part of their overall curriculum. Both B'nai B'rith's A World of Difference, which teaches students to break down prejudice, racism, and stereotyping, and The Institute for Character Education, which is a comprehensive curriculum, are among the best and most popular of these curricula.

To teach moral values, some schools encourage students to actively participate in the school's governing, from decisions about school policy to disciplining their peers. In this way, students learn responsibility and civic duty firsthand.

A few schools have adopted a "community service" concept, similar to the program of the American Ethical Union's high school, the Fieldston School. For example, junior high students in Minneapolis shovel snow for the disabled, read to the blind, and help nursing home residents balance their checkbooks.[30] In Rye, New York, high school students need sixty hours of community service in order to graduate. They perform this service on weekends, during summer vacation, or during free periods in the school day.

Said Bana Mouwakeh, a senior at Rye High School, who volunteered two hundred hours in a hospital and another two hundred in a soup kitchen: "The first time I went to the soup kitchen, I was very scared and uncomfortable. But the homeless have beautiful stories to tell and meaningful things to say. I look forward to it everytime I go now."[31]

William Damon, author of *The Moral Child*, suggests inviting "moral mentors" into the school, much the way artists and writers now come.[32] "Leaders in sheltering the homeless, healing the sick, caring for abandoned children, and so on," suggests Damon, should discuss their work. Such discussions would "inspire students to assume genuine moral responsibility." Schools like the Lab School at the University of Chicago have already taken the lead in this approach.

The School of Life

Families, religion, and schools are not the only moral instructors. Children learn from many other sources—from movies and television to games and friends. Troubling, though, is how many of these are filled with messages of violence and poor moral standards. Also disturbing is how many popular sports figures, entertainers, and other celebrities exemplify negative values, such as getting ahead at all costs, materialism, and selfishness.

It is easy to look at pop culture and its messengers and question their effectiveness at moral teaching. But hope is on the horizon.

After the armored car incident in Columbus, Ohio, which is described in chapter one, the mayor appointed a Commission on Ethics and Morals to remind citizens in Columbus of the importance of honesty and other moral values. Through a public relations campaign called "Take an Honest Look," honesty was highlighted throughout the year in spots on TV and radio, on billboards, in newspaper articles, and through other publicity.

Many television and radio stations air programs that discuss ethics, including talk shows, news magazine shows, after-school specials, and public television's ten-part series, *Ethics in America*. Some popular movies also carry positive moral messages.

Even the nightly news sometimes brings hope and moral inspiration. Whether it is an outpouring of support for disaster victims of air crashes, hurricanes, or earthquakes, or the less dramatic attention accorded to a Nobel Peace Prize winner, moral education abounds.

When Mahatma Gandhi, India's beloved leader in the struggle for independence from England, was asked why he had changed his views over the course of a week, he explained, "Because I have learned something since last week."[33]

It is important to maintain perspective and balance on the goals of moral education. As Alice Miller reflects, "Where do you find humans who are *only* good or *only* cruel?"[34] After all, while we all "miss the mark" at times, most of us do not become agents of evil and destruction.

Achieving moral perfection is an impossible goal. But like Gandhi, we can always continue to learn more. Ironically, if we have been poorly taught, learning moral behavior may require undoing those teachings. Or when we fail to learn our moral lessons it may require repeating them—again and again.

5

EVEN HEROES HAVE FEET OF CLAY

Pete Rose enjoyed one of the most outstanding careers in baseball history. With his cocky manner and legendary swing, he was the best player on one of the best teams—the Cincinnati Reds. He had a record 4256 hits, was baseball's first million-dollar singles hitter, and, at forty, was still batting .325.[1]

Then on August 29, 1990, when he learned that Rose had placed bets on baseball games, baseball commissioner A. Bartlett Giamatti suspended Rose from playing baseball—for life.[2] Less then a year later, a federal judge convicted Rose of filing false income tax returns and sentenced him to five months in prison, three months parole, one thousand hours of community service, and a fifty-thousand-dollar fine.[3]

Despite his conviction and sentence, Pete Rose's batting record remained intact, as well as his desire for a place in the Baseball Hall of Fame. But his reputation was tarnished.

"I made mistakes everyday," Rose told a reporter.

"Hell, I lost a seven-hundred-and-fifty-thousand-dollar-a-year job."[4] And to the judge at the U.S. district court who sentenced him, he said these words: "I lost my dignity. I lost my self-respect. I lost a lot of dear fans and almost lost some very dear friends. Somewhere, somehow, I hope to make it up to everybody that I disappointed and let down."[5]

Pete Rose attributed his mistakes to chronic gambling. If he could have foreseen the consequences of his wrongdoings, he would have sought help for his addiction before it ruined his career. But although he traced his problem to gambling, others regarded his problem as a lack of *character*. Explaining why Rose is ineligible for election to the Baseball Hall of Fame, Lee MacPhail, a former president of the American League, said: "The rules for election to the Hall cite integrity, character, and sportsmanship . . . someone on the ineligible list does not meet those qualifications."[6]

Building Character

Ethics is not just how we think and act. It is also about *character*. The values, principles, and moral rules by which we live; the scruples that stop us from doing wrong; and the way we act—all of these make up our character.

Even though other people can strongly influence us, we alone have the power to build, change, or destroy our character.

Character is "built" thought by thought, act by act, deed by deed. As you accumulate good thoughts and behavior, you build good character, and as you accumulate bad ones, you erode or destroy your character. Eventually, the cumulative effects of these thoughts and behavior give you your character. In turn, it also defines who you are. And with character you earn the trust—or mistrust—of others. And with that, you earn your reputation, or what others think of you.

Falling from Grace

What others say about you—whether or not it is truthful—can destroy your reputation. And like Humpty Dumpty, reputations can't always be completely restored. In contrast, because character is within our own control it can be restored (though not easily).

Character is more than simply adding and subtracting your deeds and misdeeds. You can do something wrong and still maintain good character. We refer to such wrongdoings as "out of character," precisely because they are not consistent with a person's moral standards or usual conduct.

If you *continue* doing wrong, however gradually, your character changes. (Likewise, if you continue doing good, you can change bad character too.)

Down the Slippery Slope

As Pete Rose learned, people can lose their reputation overnight. But character changes more slowly, usually beginning as a gradual descent down a "slippery slope" of wrongdoing.

Lying or cheating once, or even twice, does not make you a "liar" or a "cheater." Each time you do it, though, it becomes easier to repeat. With each episode, you learn to overcome the fear and guilt that keep you from habitually lying and cheating. In time, it becomes so easy that you may cease to see lying or cheating as wrong. By then, your character is strikingly different from before.

For example, most hardened criminals do not start out committing serious crimes. Rather, as adolescents, they tend to begin with small ones. Little by little, in increments, they overcome their inhibitions and "slide down the slippery slope" to more serious crime. On the other hand, each time we avoid immoral behavior, even in small ways, we find it easier to be a moral person. This is how virtues, or good habits, are developed.

As we established in the previous chapter, we learn moral conduct from many sources. Learning from our mistakes is still another way—probably the most effective, but also the most painful.

In 1990 Rob Pilatus and Fab Morvan, the charismatic stars of the pop duo Milli Vanilli, were riding the huge crest of fame and success. Their hit album, *Girl, You Know It's True,* sold 7 million records in the United States and 22 million worldwide.[7] Equally impressive sales from videos, cassettes, CDs, other merchandise, and concert appearances earned them a fortune, plus adulation from fans and respect from fellow musicians. That same year the music industry awarded them the Grammy for Outstanding Newcomer.

Then rumors and an incident in which their equipment briefly failed during a concert led to a confession from the dreadlocked duo that their talent was not just break dancing. It was also lip-synching and deception: They didn't really sing on their albums or at their concerts. The Grammy was taken back, and the duo was publicly disgraced.

"We realize exactly what we did to achieve our success," Pilatus admitted during a two-hour interview after the hoax was exposed. "We made some big mistakes and we apologize. And we hope to make it up."[8]

Earning back their fans' and their industry's trust would be difficult. But through their ordeal, the two had the opportunity to learn something about moral wisdom and the value of integrity.

Signposts Along the Way

Just as our conscience regulates us along the moral way, warning us *before* we act, signposts of a different nature teach us afterward. Pride and self-respect for something done right (or for avoiding something wrong) reinforce our good behavior. Similarly, shame and guilt signal that we've done something wrong—and signal us not to repeat our misdeed.

According to Joan Borysenko, research scientist

and author of *Guilt Is the Teacher, Love Is the Lesson*, there are two kinds of guilt—healthy and unhealthy.[9]

Healthy guilt occurs when we feel remorseful about something we have done wrong. With healthy guilt, advises Borysenko, we can take responsibility for our mistake, talk about and learn from it, make the appropriate restitution, then "let it go."

Unhealthy guilt, in contrast, is what Martin Seligman, a psychologist at the University of Pennsylvania, calls "psychological pessimism."[10] It is guilt you feel even though you have done nothing morally wrong to deserve it. Many victims of crime, for example, feel unhealthy guilt, as if the crime were their fault. Sometimes sole survivors of disasters feel unhealthy guilt, blaming themselves for surviving when others did not.

Moral responsibility means we take the blame for what we've done wrong. It does not require feeling guilty or shameful for someone else's wrongdoing, even those whom we love and with whom we closely identify.

Learning to live with healthy guilt and getting rid of unhealthy guilt are both challenges. Meeting these challenges may require help, such as prayer, therapy, or talking to someone you trust about the guilt.

Facing the Music

After his service station was robbed, Dave Pasterek did not believe he'd ever make up his loss. But then, he received this letter in the mail: "I am sorry. I drank too much and broke into your station on a dare. I am sorry." In the envelope with the letter were the $167 in cash and all $1600 worth of checks and credit card receipts that had been stolen.[11]

Ethics requires moral *culpability*—that we own up to our behavior by accepting blame for it and taking responsibility for our mistakes and wrongdoings. (From a religious viewpoint, this means acknowledging our sins.)

Owning up to your misdeeds takes courage and humility. It also gives you a second chance to make good and come clean. For character is also built by accepting responsibility for our mistakes.

This means, first of all, that you acknowledge your wrongdoing and apologize for your misbehavior. But "sorry" is not enough. To live morally, you are expected to right your wrongs, or at least do your best to compensate for any harm or injustice you have caused or done. This is called restitution.

Historically, "an eye for an eye and a tooth for a tooth" was the standard retribution for a wrongdoing. What you did to wrong someone else, that person could do to you, and vice versa.

For their legal wrongs, people are expected to "pay for their crimes." Through fines and punishment, our legal system provides for retribution. Through programs like community service, for example, our government gives lawbreakers the opportunity to redress their crimes.

Wanting to get back at someone for hurting you or treating you unfairly is natural. But two wrongs don't always add up to a moral right. Morality is not necessarily a balancing act. The greater good may require meeting someone more than halfway. And the loss that someone suffers is often more than the remorse expressed by the wrongdoer or the punishment extracted from him or her can equal.

How can anyone begin to compensate for gossip that ruins a fine reputation? How can drunk drivers compensate the loss of those they kill? How can rapists compensate for the trauma they put their victims through?

By apologizing, asking for forgiveness, and—most of all—by taking responsibility and trying what we *can* to redress a misdeed, we attempt to right our wrongs. Above all, we right them by learning not to repeat them.

With the best intentions, we make mistakes and do things we later regret. Even for the worst mistakes, we can repent and try to change our ways. After learning from our mistakes, forgiveness is the way we move on with our lives.

Forgiveness is not the same as forgetting. It is impossible to intentionally forget a wrong, especially a serious one. Remembering, in fact, is what keeps us from repeating our mistakes or enables us to prevent them from happening again.

Nor is forgiveness a substitute for anger. It is natural to get angry at others and ourselves for harm or injustice. Sometimes our anger is good or morally right. Sometimes it is excessive or morally wrong.

But whether the anger itself is right or wrong, how we express it is morally important too.

Since so many of our moral lessons are learned from our mistakes, learning how to forgive ourselves for making them, and to forgive others as well, is as important as learning how to be moral in the first place.

Mending Our Ways

It can be too late to repair the damage you do, but it is never too late to mend your ways, change your behavior, and try to improve your character or your reputation.

John Newton was born to a seafaring family in England in 1725.[12] When his mother died, his father secured him a job at sea. Newton so despised the job that he ran away, only to be forced into naval duty, from which he also escaped. Finally, he did end up at sea—as a commander of slave-trading ships.

One day, during a fierce storm in the Atlantic Ocean, Newton thought his ship was sinking and that everything would be lost. Suddenly, he exclaimed to himself, "Well, if nothing can be done, Lord, have mercy upon us!" Upon returning to his cabin for refuge from the gale winds, he thought about his words and their true meaning to him. It was then that he realized he believed in the grace of God, a revelation that changed his entire perspective on life.

Although it was a more gradual change than his sudden religious conversion, Newton eventually saw slavery as wrong. By 1754 he took his "last leave of it." The memory and horror of shipping slaves who were forced to lie in tight rows, one above the other, always remained with Newton. He remembered the slaves, "like books upon a shelf, I have known them so close that the shelf would not easily contain one more." So deeply was the image etched in his mind that he could "hardly forget or greatly mistake them."[13]

After becoming a Christian minister, Newton discussed his experiences in the slave trade. His efforts caused many influential people in London to realize that slavery was immoral, and it was ultimately outlawed there.

Sometime between 1760 and 1770, Newton composed a hymn for the parish of Olney, England, about his conversion from sinner to preacher. "Amazing Grace" is one of the most popular and inspiring hymns ever written:

> Amazing grace, how sweet the sound
> that saved a wretch like me
> I once was lost
> but now I'm found
> was blind, but now I see.

There is much evidence that shows the damage immoral behavior causes. Guarding against immorality takes a herculean effort—and monumental toll. Billions of dollars a year go toward guarding the public's welfare, from the $2 million a year the Senate Ethics Committee spends monitoring the moral behavior of our nation's leaders,[14] to the billions spent on police protection, prosecution, and incarceration.

Untold anguish, pain, and despair result from personal wrongdoing. One in every seven children is victimized by sexual abuse.[15] In many neighborhoods, it is no longer safe to live in unlocked homes or walk alone at night. And where drugs and street crime rule, even locked homes and daytime walks are unsafe. Scams and scandals abound.

But ethics is about living—and learning from our mistakes. Depending on the seriousness of a mistake, it can be too late for a second chance. We cannot always restore a good reputation to its former glory, right a wrong, or convince others and ourselves to forgive our trespasses. Nevertheless, we *can* learn from our mistakes and begin again to be the people we want to be.

6

IN THE DRIVER'S SEAT

On March 16, 1968, a company of American soldiers was dropped by helicopter into My Lai, a cluster of small hamlets in South Vietnam. There they expected to engage in battle against the 48th Viet Cong Battalion, one of their most formidable enemy units. They also assumed that pamphlets had been dropped warning any civilians to evacuate and seek refuge elsewhere.

My Lai's inhabitants never got the message. Instead, they got a day of massacre.

Nor did American troops ever find the 48th Viet Cong Battalion. Instead, they found women, children, and elderly men, many of whom were still cooking their breakfast rice or doing other morning chores.

Nevertheless, commanding officers like Lieutenant William Calley, Jr., ordered their men to open fire. In small groups in and about their homes, victims were rounded up and shot. Many were hastily thrown into ditches. Before being murdered, some of the younger women and girls were brutally raped. "We were out there . . . having a good time," explained one ex-GI to the commission later investigating the massacre. "It was sort of like a shooting gallery."[1]

After slaughtering 347 innocent Vietnamese, American soldiers systematically burned each home, destroyed all livestock and food, and fouled the area's drinking supply.[2]

Out of hatred for the Viet Cong and desire for revenge, most of the GIs initially tried to justify their actions. "I felt like I was doing the right thing," explained one GI, "because . . . I lost buddies. I lost a damn good buddy, Bobby Wilson, and it was on my conscience. So after I done it, I felt good, but later on that day, it was getting to me."[3]

To most, however, it never occurred that they had a moral responsibility *not* to participate—or even a choice. "I felt I was ordered to do it," was a familiar response.[4]

Even afterward no one involved took responsibility for what had happened. From majors on down, the massacre was cleverly concealed and reported as a military victory. Only when ex-GI Ronald Ridenhour (who was uninvolved in the massacre but had heard about it) wrote to President Lyndon B. Johnson, the Pentagon, twenty-four congressmen, reporters, and others was it exposed and brought to trial.[5]

The scientist and writer C. P. Snow observed that obedience can override all that we know about ethics and moral conduct, as well as what we feel for others. "When you think of the long and gloomy history of man," he wrote, "you will find more hideous crimes have been committed in the name of obedience than have even been committed in the name of rebellion."[6]

To Thine Own Self Be True

To preserve the social order we need for living together harmoniously, obedience and respect for authority are necessary. (Although they are in the minority, some philosophers even argue that because social order is so vital to protecting society, we should, in fact, blindly follow authority.)

Imagine what would happen if a sizeable number of people disregarded traffic laws. Speed limits and traffic lights would become meaningless. Although traveling might be faster at times, especially on lightly traveled roads, chaos would ensue at busy intersections and thoroughfares.

Imagine, too, a classroom with no respect for the teacher. Doing what you want might be fun at first, but soon the noise and disruption would render teaching and learning impossible.

Nevertheless, as the tragedy of My Lai shows, authority should not be blindly followed. It is important to question orders and decisions that go against your conscience, and to take responsibility for whatever you do choose to follow.

Philosophers such as Thomas Hobbes argued that only those in authority (like Lieutenant Calley) are morally responsible for the orders they give, and not the people who follow them.[7] However, most ethicists sharply disagree. They believe that ethics puts the moral responsibility on everyone—those giving the orders *and* those carrying them out.

It follows that ethics requires you to make your own decisions about right and wrong, and to obey your own conscience, not someone else's. Or as Shakespeare's Polonius advised: "To thine own self be true."

For this you must be *free* to choose, to make your own moral decisions and take your own actions—be they moral *or* immoral. Such freedom to choose and make moral decisions is called *moral agency* or *moral autonomy*.

Choosing moral autonomy and following your conscience during a military ambush like My Lai is an extreme example—and very difficult to do. For war depends on obedience to superiors, and those who defy orders usually suffer serious reprisal; they are court-martialed or even killed.

Nor are people who are unable to make moral decisions held morally responsible for their behavior. A person who is insane, for example, and unable to think clearly cannot make moral decisions and cannot be held morally responsible for his or her behavior.

Yet people who can think clearly and are in far less stressful situations than war and ambush often fail to exercise moral autonomy. Some even deny they have any.

In the Driver's Seat

Moral autonomy is so important that many religions have ceremonies marking when members are ready to assume it. In Judaism this event is called a bar or bat mitzvah (in Hebrew, *bar* means boy, while *bat* means girl.) In some Christian denominations, there is also a ceremony at adolescence, called a confirmation. Still other Christian denominations recognize baptism as the ceremony marking moral agency.

Despite such rites of moral passage, adults and teenagers often disagree on when teenagers are mature enough to make certain moral decisions for themselves, or handle the consequences of their decisions. As a result, they disagree on when to allow teens the moral autonomy to make those decisions.

The right to make your own decisions usually depends on the situation, your parents' attitudes, and the laws in the state where you live. Each year, for example, a million teenagers get pregnant.[8] Who determines whether or not a teenager is ready for single parenthood or marriage, or should place a baby in foster care or give it up for adoption? Who decides when a teenager can make the decision to have an abortion or give birth?

Many teenagers seek their parents' support and advice during such crises. Many have the moral autonomy to make such decisions. However, not all teenagers do.

In most states, until they are eighteen, teenagers

cannot choose to marry without either a parent's or guardian's consent.[9]

While all states allow teenagers to choose to have a baby, many states deny them the right to choose abortion. At least twenty-three states require a parent's or judge's approval to give a teenager the moral autonomy to make the decision herself.[10]

In most situations, you earn moral freedom by accepting responsibility for your behavior, showing you have good judgment, and proving that you can be trusted. Or you attain it by exercising it anyway, as the following example shows.

When Kristen's friend Melissa bragged about babysitting for a two-year-old whose diaper she'd remove to fondle his penis, Kristen was shocked.[11] Because she knew how wrong Melissa's behavior was, she faced a moral dilemma. If she squealed on her friend, Melissa would get into serious trouble (and perhaps ruin her friendship with Kristen as well). After days of worrying, Kristen decided to seek her parents' advice.

Yet when she told them what was happening, she encountered still another critical decision to make. For they not only warned her not to get involved, they assured her they had no intention of getting involved either. "It's none of our business," they said.

Should I obey or disobey? thought Kristen. After much anguish, she decided to disobey them, and reported the incident to a woman she knew who was involved in a sexual abuse prevention program. As a result, Kristen's friend was treated by a psychiatrist, the toddler's parents were informed, and Kristen's parents never discovered what had transpired. (Not all reports end on such a positive note, however.)

Kristen had the courage to follow her conscience and take responsibility. Her conduct is inspiring, but not always easy to emulate. In a classic experiment at Yale University, social psychologist Stanley Milgram demonstrated how difficult defying authority is.[12]

Milgram's subjects were ordinary people—salesmen, postal clerks, engineers, teachers and laborers—who answered an advertisement to get paid for participating in a pioneering study at Yale University.

Each subject was informed that the purpose of the experiment was to study the effects of punishment on learning. What Milgram was really studying, though, was the extent to which the subjects would obey someone in authority who told them to inflict painful electric shocks on a person who neither threatened nor hurt them.

At the start of the experiment, a professional-looking researcher appeared, dressed in a gray technician's coat. He instructed the subject to teach another "subject," a mild-mannered accountant, a list of word pairs. Every time the accountant made a mistake, the subject was to punish him with an electric shock, triggered by pulling a lever on an impressive-looking shock generator. Moreover, with each subsequent mistake, the subject was told to increase the shock by pulling the next lever on the machine.

There were thirty levers, ranging from 15 to 450 volts. Switches were marked from SLIGHT SHOCK to DANGER-SEVERE SHOCK, while the highest was simply labeled xxx.

All the subjects believed that they were actually shocking the other man. In reality, however, the learner, or victim, was an actor who received no shock at all.

At 75 volts, the "learner" grunted; at 120 volts, he complained that it hurt. At increasingly higher voltage levels, he screamed and shouted, "Let me out of here! My heart's bothering me. Let me out! Let me out!" At the highest voltage level, his screams could only be described as agonized.

As the experiment wore on, subjects grew exceedingly uncomfortable when issuing the shocks and hearing the victim's protests and outbursts of pain. They sweated, trembled, laughed nervously, bit their lips, or even dug their fingernails into their flesh.

Often they turned to the researcher to ask for advice or permission to stop. Always the researcher said, in a nonthreatening but authoritative tone, "The experiment requires that you continue," or later, "You have no other choice, you *must* go on."

At what point would the subject refuse to obey? Despite the protests and anguished screams, despite the fact that they were never forced or bribed to continue, despite the fact that they wanted desperately to quit, despite how wrong they believed it was to hurt innocent people, the majority of subjects—65 percent—delivered the full range of shocks, including the 450-volt shock marked xxx. Why?

Relatively few people can defy authority. Others become so absorbed in a task that they lose sight of the broader consequences. Rather than accept responsibility themselves, still others shift the responsibility for any wrongdoing to those who issued the orders in the first place.

The most far-reaching consequence of obedience, Milgram concluded, was that of giving up your moral autonomy and responsibility for your actions. Trying to justify their actions, many of his subjects responded, "I wouldn't have done it by myself," or "I was just doing what I was told."[13]

The key to morality is our right to choose it. We don't always agree with those in authority, nor should we. But the challenge is to gain moral autonomy when we deserve it—and when we have it, to use it.

7

CHOOSING FROM THE MORAL MENU

In Robert Coles' book *The Spiritual Life of Children*, a young Hopi girl explains why her tribe's moral outlook is so different from the "Anglo's." "The sky watches us," she explained, "and listens to us. It talks to us, and it hopes we are ready to talk back. The sky is where the God of the Anglos lives, a teacher told us. She asked where our God lives. I said, 'I don't know.' I was telling the truth! Our God is the sky and lives wherever the sky is. Our God is the sun and the moon, too; and our God is the Hopi people, if we remember to stay here on our land.

"A long time ago," she continued, "our people spoke to the Anglos and told them what we think, but they don't listen to hear *us;* they listen to hear themselves. My grandmother says they live to conquer the sky and we live to pray for it, and you can't explain yourself to people who conquer."[1]

Usually we think we know right from wrong. But explaining the moral theory behind it—*why* something is right or wrong—is complicated. As Judith Jarvis Thomson, author of many critical essays on ethics, observes, "Nobody expects chemistry or physics to be simple. Why do so many people expect moral theory to be simple?

"Ethics is complicated because there is no end to the range of possible situations in which humans may find themselves, nor to the range of beliefs, intentions, and motives they act on in those situations."[2]

Navigating Through Life

Like the ancient sailors who used the North Star to guide their way across vast oceans and seas, we guide ourselves through moral mazes with a *moral compass*. Our moral compass, or moral outlook, consists of the principles, values, priorities, and goals that we use to determine our morality. It's the "voice" behind our moral reasoning, the moral theory behind our actions. When we listen to our conscience, our moral compass gives us "whys" and "why-nots."

People don't simply choose their moral compass. Their moral values are influenced by what their parents, teachers, and others have taught them—or failed to teach them. When we choose to act in accordance with those values, we are following our moral compass.

As you learn more about ethics and life, your moral compass may change, especially after going through a tragic accident or disease. With new experiences, many people acquire different values and, with them, a new moral compass. A moral compass is supposed to point the way toward truth and moral goodness. If it doesn't, it may lead the way to trouble—not only for yourself but for society as well when others share the same troublesome moral compass.

During the 1980s, for example, many Wall Street brokers traded in bonds that were risky, but enormously profitable. In one year junk-bond investor Michael Milken earned over half a billion dollars.[3]

Driven by greed, Milken and investors like him used illegal means to grow even wealthier by using inside information unavailable to public stockholders. As a result, thousands of them lost substantial investments—to the tune of millions, if not billions, of dollars. In fact, some of Milken's staunchest critics also blame him for the demise of hundreds of businesses and the loss of thousands of jobs.[4] When Milken was finally convicted of his crimes, he received a harsh penalty—$600 million in fines, ten years in prison, three years probation, and 5400 hours of community service.[5]

Vive la Différence

All moral compasses are not the same. Some are more universal than others. This means that their moral rules apply to everyone under all circumstances.

An example of a universal moral law is the Golden Rule. As a moral compass, the Golden Rule can apply to any moral situation: *Always* do unto others as you would have them do unto you.

Some religious groups have universal rules about abortion. Under all circumstances—including rape or incest—abortion is viewed as wrong. If they believe the rule was revealed by God—divine revelation—they consider it unchangeable—morally certain and inarguable. According to their belief, abortion is wrong in and of itself.

Immanuel Kant, a German philosopher who lived during the eighteenth century, believed that a moral compass could be reduced to one universal law governing all of morality.[6] Calling this law a *categorical imperative*, he stated it this way: "Act so that you can simultaneously will that the maxim of your action should become universal law." In other words, don't do anything unless you would want anyone else in the same circumstances to do the same thing. For example, according to Kant's categorical imperative, lying is always wrong because we could not will that it be universally practiced. Likewise, sneaking into the movies is wrong because if it was universally practiced—if everyone did it—movie theaters would go bankrupt.

A different view contends that in most situations there are usually several moral rules in conflict with one another. Which rule you obey depends upon the situation. For example, a situation may involve a conflict between being honest and avoiding harm. It might be right to lie in order to protect someone from harm; protecting someone's life might be more valuable than being honest.

Your opinion of the source of moral truth—where right or wrong comes from—is another major part of your moral compass. One opinion is that moral truth is absolute and unchangeable—"it is, because it is." Here, there are fundamental truths, a "natural law" containing certain moral values that human beings can discover and know.

In marked contrast is the opinion that moral truth is relative—to a culture, a personal ideal, a legal or economic system—"it all depends." When morality is relative and linked to different interpretations of moral truth, a decision or behavior that is moral in one society may be considered immoral in another. For example, in a conservative culture like Saudi Arabia, giving birth to a child out of wedlock is taboo and harshly condemned. But in liberal Sweden it is morally acceptable. Likewise, when moral truth is relative to personal beliefs, two people are apt to view the same situation quite differently.

Tradition, Tradition

Many traditions feed into our Western approach to making ethical decisions. Ethicist Lisa Newton defined four major, overlapping ones:[7]

1. Greek quest for excellence, emphasizing cultivation of virtue and character;
2. Judeo-Christian biblical commitment to God—to obey God's laws and to love God and neighbor;
3. Moral law tradition that includes a range of thought about natural laws and the natural rights of human beings;
4. Utilitarian tradition, which strives for the pur-

suit of greatest happiness for the greatest number in the long run.

Along with these four traditions are influences from other traditions. Eastern philosophy's Zen and yoga, and Native-American spirituality contribute much to environmental ethics by teaching respect and dignity for the whole earth.

Twentieth-century French philosopher Jean-Paul Sartre wrote several books that reflected his theory of *existentialism*; this theory explained much of the anxiety and alienation that modern people were feeling. Sartre believed that the universe is absurd, and that people have absolute freedom of choice, including the freedom to determine their own moral code.

Understanding all the different moral theories and traditions requires an astute, scholarly mind. In our effort to discover what is right and wrong, however, theories and tradition can be extremely helpful.

Despite their differences, all moral traditions address the same basic questions:

What is the purpose of living?
What is the "moral good"?
How can we live a life that has purpose and achieve the moral good?

Your moral compass, or outlook, determines how you answer these.

In Christian tradition, the purpose of living is to honor God and be God's faithful steward.[8] Many

Eastern religions define the purpose of living as attaining eternal salvation, freeing oneself from the bondage of birth and rebirth, or finding spiritual grace.

In the Greek tradition, Plato defined the moral good in terms of virtues like wisdom, courage, temperance, and justice. Immanuel Kant claimed that the only "unconditional good" is the goodwill residing within a rational person.

From the utilitarian tradition, John Stuart Mill defined the moral good as the "greatest good for the greatest number of people." Consequently, if hard work and decent incomes give the majority of people happiness and well-being, then the opportunity to work and earn a decent living is a moral good.

To achieve the moral good, Aristotle suggested the "Golden Mean"—acting with moderation, never in the extreme. The Italian philosopher Saint Thomas Aquinas taught that the moral good can only be achieved with behavior that is motivated by love.

How you define the moral good is important because it determines how you set your moral course—what goals you strive for and what priorities you value. For example, people who value self-interest set a very different course from those who value justice. The former are inclined to choose careers that advance their financial status and power, while the latter are more inclined to choose helping or teaching professions.

Choosing from the Moral Menu

As we have just discussed, the moral menu offers a potpourri of moral theories taken from different traditions. Following is a sample of some of those theories:

The ends justify the means. For four years, Marilyn Louise Harrell, a private escrow agent for the federal government's Department of Housing and Urban Development, diverted as much as $5.5 million from H.U.D. to feed, clothe, and shelter the poor in the suburbs of Washington, D.C.[9] She bought twenty houses and forty cars, created a charity called Friends of the Father, and provided seed money to start four businesses that employed the indigent.

"There were so many hurting people," Harrell explained. "We bought them groceries. We paid their electric and gas bills so they could be warm. We paid their rent."

Like the legendary Robin Hood, with the best of intentions Marilyn Harrell stole from the rich to help the poor. Is there anything wrong with that?

"From Machiavelli to Marx, utilitarians have been arguing that the end justifies the means," wrote feminist Gloria Steinem in an article on ethics. Like other critics of utilitarianism, Steinem concludes that it is self-defeating. "Whatever means you use will *become* part of the ends you achieve."[10]

How you can get there determines where you go. This moral compass determines how we obtain what we strive for. Indian leader Mahatma Gandhi, for example, strove to attain India's freedom from England. But he believed that the only way to reach the goal of freedom was through nonviolence. "I would not kill for freedom," explained Gandhi, "but I am willing to die for it."

In a similar vein, some people are more concerned about how they can live a morally good life than about the material goals they achieve. Viktor Frankl, author of *Man's Search for Meaning*, illustrated this when he advised not to aim for success as a goal. "The more you aim at it and make it a target," he wrote, "the more you are going to miss it. For success, like happiness, cannot be pursued; it must ensue, and it only does so as the unintended side-effect of one's personal dedication to a cause greater than oneself or as the by-product of one's surrender to a person other than oneself."[11] Happiness must happen, and the same holds true for success—you have to let it happen by not caring about it.

If it's legal, it must be moral. Laws have always had a strong connection to morality. In writing the Declaration of Independence, Thomas Jefferson tied law and morality together when he wrote: "We hold these truths to be self-evident, that all men are created equal, that they are endowed by their Creator with certain unalienable Rights, that among these are Life, Liberty and the pursuit of happiness."

A desire to respect and obey the law is good. But not every law that reflects a society's moral code is moral, as laws that have legalized slavery, segregation, sexism, or apartheid—all immoral—prove. Such laws can never justify such behavior.

Inspired by the writings of Saint Thomas Aquinas, a thirteenth-century monk and philosopher, Martin Luther King, Jr., addressed this issue in a letter he wrote from jail in Birmingham, Alabama, during the Civil Rights movement. "Any law that uplifts human personality is just. Any law that degrades human personality is unjust."[12]

On that premise, Dr. King never advocated taking the law into your own hands or disobeying a just law. "That would lead to anarchy," he said. To teach others how unjust a law is, Dr. King advised, it is moral to break that law if you are willing to accept the consequences of breaking it, including imprisonment. In fact, he believed that such actions "expressed the highest respect" for our legal system.[13]

Laws usually reflect a society's moral code. Laws prohibiting prostitution, for example, reflect a moral code that believes selling sex is wrong. Some people, however, want to write more of the moral code into law. According to them, if an action is moral, it should be legal, and if it is immoral, it should be illegal. But issues like school prayer, abortion, gambling, or gun control evoke such intense moral debate and so little agreement that it is difficult to rely solely on the legal system as a litmus test for their morality or immorality.

Because it feels good. From the Greek philosopher Epicurus to twentieth-century author Ayn

Rand, some philosophers believe that all moral behavior is motivated by self-interest. If it feels good, it must be right.

As we have learned about empathy and altruism, feeling good does inspire many people to do good. But a desire to feel good also inspires others to behave selfishly. Michael Josephson, founder and director of the Joseph and Edna Josephson Institute of Ethics, labels such "me-first" adherents as IDIs—"I-deserve-its."[14]

At its extreme, hedonism, or doing whatever you please, is hurtful and unjust. Moreover, thinking they can do anything they please, as long as they don't get caught, leads many people to corruption and moral decay.

The Bible tells me so. In the West, one of the most influential and widely accepted moral compasses comes from the Judeo-Christian tradition. Throughout the Bible and other religious texts are commandments and prescriptions for moral living.

From the biblical outlook comes two basic moral commitments.[15] The earliest commitment is to justice. In the Old Testament, a sign of righteousness is how well a people care for the weakest members of their community; taking advantage of anyone weaker than oneself for personal gain is always wrong.[16]

The other important commitment is to love God. Out of that love and desire to serve God comes love of neighbor. "You shall love the Lord with all your soul, and with all your strength, and with all your mind; and your neighbor as yourself."[17]

Shifting Tides

Moral *inconsistency* appears to be part of human nature, and especially part of childhood. In research on thousands of children, psychologists Hugh Hartshorne and Mark May studied moral conduct, such as cheating, lying, and stealing.[18] They found little consistency among children. For example, while in church many children reported being honest. But if they were in a clubhouse or other nonreligious setting, the same children would often change their moral compass and admit to dishonesty.

Many ethicists believe it is important to keep the same moral compass until you need or find a better one. (After all, bad moral compasses lead to bad behavior.) If you are morally consistent, others learn to trust or mistrust you. Abraham Lincoln was so consistently honest, for example, that he earned the trust of others along with the nickname "Honest Abe."

In contrast, during a seminar for state legislative leaders, one participant tried to reason that because he was honest most of the time, he deserved to be trusted as a basically honest person. Michael Josephson, the seminar leader and founder of the Joseph and Edna Josephson Institute of Ethics, disagreed. Explaining the importance of moral consistency in building trust and confidence, he said: "You only have to lie to a person *once* to be considered a liar. You could tell the person, 'Wait, but I told you the truth twenty times!' But it doesn't sell, does it?"[19]

Moral inconsistency is hypocritical. When television ministers Jimmy Lee Swaggart and Jim Bakker preached monogamy and then committed adultery, their hypocrisy betrayed their followers and perhaps even the public's trust in the ministry. For in just two years, from 1988 to 1990, public trust of the clergy dropped significantly.[20] And when Dana Rinehart, the mayor of Columbus, Ohio, who had launched a citywide campaign on ethics, admitted to lying to reporters about an affair he had with one of his cabinet members, he too betrayed the public's confidence in him and eroded its trust.[21]

Understanding the different moral compasses is a challenge. It requires a sophisticated knowledge of philosophy and religion, as well as an ability to think logically.

But many people who are ignorant of Socrates' *Crito*, Immanuel Kant's categorical imperative, or John Rawls' *A Theory of Justice*, and other ethical traditions live morally rich, even saintly lives.

According to Samuel and Pearl Oliner, authors of *The Altruistic Personality*, "Most people become virtuous because of their deep connection and abiding respect for the world and those who live in it."[22] Through such "rootedness" and camaraderie, these people navigate through life as well as the best Ph.D.s in philosophy—maybe even better. For the greatest challenge is not philosophical understanding, but rather moral living.

8

A DIFFERENCE
OF OPINION

When twelve-year-old Pamela Hamilton broke her leg, the chiropractor who x-rayed it found a tumor that was later diagnosed as Ewing's sarcoma, a rare and deadly form of bone cancer. The tumor grew to the size of a watermelon. Even with chemotherapy, Pamela's doctor gave her a one in four chance of surviving. Because of a deeply held religious belief that only God, not doctors, can heal, Pamela opposed any medical treatment.[1]

Pamela's father and mother supported her decision to refuse treatment, and fought for it legally when doctors took them to court. Her case raises many ethical questions. Does a twelve-year-old have the right to make a decision that may cost her her life? Does freedom of religion include the right to withhold conventional medical treatment from children? (Legally, it does not, but we are asking whether or not it morally does.)

In contrast, Leanne Black, also a teenager, suffered from the same rare form of bone cancer as Pamela Hamilton. For several years she had chemotherapy, and when that failed, she underwent amputation of her leg. "God has nothing to do with the cure of cancer," said Leanne in response to Pamela's decision to refuse medical treatment. "Chemotherapy and the doctors do. . . . I think her decision is wrong . . . chemotherapy will prolong her life . . . and a twenty-five percent chance of living . . . well, that's better than nothing."[2]

Who is right, Pamela or Leanne? Despite their difference of opinion, can they *both* be right?

In America we have the freedom to think whatever we like. With our diverse backgrounds, we approach ethics differently and have strong opinions about certain moral issues. Ethical inquiry requires that we maintain a healthy respect for opinions that are different from our own, that we learn to understand and tolerate them. It also raises important questions. How do we know which side is right and which is wrong? In particular situations, is there even a right or wrong?

As ethicist Lisa Newton contends, "Ethics is not like mathematics, where there is one right answer. There can be honest and possibly irreconcilable disagreement."

Even though there are differences, she believes that there *are* better and worse answers. "If there weren't," says Newton, "it wouldn't be worth the effort to reflect on matters of ethics . . . and attempt to reach valid conclusions on one's own."[3]

Given all the diverging viewpoints, is it possible to tolerate moral beliefs and behavior that are different from our own, especially if we think they are wrong? For example, can vegetarians allow hunting on their property? Can a person who supports the right to abortion vote for a candidate who opposes abortion? Can someone who has liberal views of sexuality tolerate someone who doesn't?

Sometimes the balancing act occurs within ourselves. Are we hypocrites if we worry about ecology and use disposable diapers? Or take a firm stand against nuclear weapons, then work for a defense company that manufactures parts for them?

The most effective way to tolerate differences is to appreciate and understand the reasons for them. In both public forums and private conversations, we discuss and debate different moral viewpoints to reach compromise or at least greater tolerance.

Newspaper editorials and essays, letters to the editor, and many fine books discuss moral differences. Television programs, professional conferences, and educational seminars also sponsor such discussions.

For instance, in 1988, Ted Koppel, the host of *Nightline*, held a discussion on legalizing drugs and invited experts from all sides of the issue onto the program. During a two-day congressional hearing only a month later, Representative Charles Rangel, chairman of the House Select Committee on Narcotics Abuse and Control, continued the debate, hearing both advocates and opponents of legalization explain its merits and pitfalls.[4]

Learning How to Listen

Tolerance requires good communication. Only by careful listening and respect for the opinion of others can you gain insight, clarity, and a broader perspective. It helps to concede—if only to yourself—that the other viewpoint *may* be better than yours, or at least that you *both* may be wrong. It also helps not to perceive the other side as an "enemy" or an "opponent," but rather as a person with good intentions, albeit with a different viewpoint.

Such discussion opens you up to criticism—and change. Given the opportunity to learn more and gain a new perspective, you may change your opinion or behavior.

Some people will not listen to any other viewpoints besides their own. Instead of having a give-and-take discussion, they merely speak their mind, refusing to hear any other arguments. Or by limiting their discussion only to people with similar ideas, they avoid hearing opposing arguments altogether. Unfortunately, such attitudes deny them the healthy exchange that fosters understanding and tolerance. They are also denied the opportunity to bridge the gap between divergent ideas. These differences can often escalate into animosity, fear, resentment, and anger. And sometimes they even incite violence.

In 1989, on a *Geraldo* show about racism, a guest espousing white supremacy accused another guest of being an "Uncle Tom." Instead of discussing the issue, tempers flared. The guest accused of being an Uncle Tom punched his accuser in the face. Fighting quickly broke out among all of the guests. The melee even involved host Rivera, who suffered a broken nose.

Stretching Too Far

There are limits to tolerance. In fact, when conduct is unreasonable or morally reprehensible, *in*tolerance may be justifiable.

In the small town of Moe, Australia, a couple was so financially strapped that they resorted to putting one of their sons up for sale.[5] At their local shopping center, Phillip and Judith Walther posted notices to sell either twenty-month-old Benjamin, four-year-old Andrew, or seven-year-old David. During a television interview, Phillip Walther explained that he needed to fetch no less than fifteen thousand dollars in order to pay his debts.

Cases like this raise concerns about child abuse and financial desperation. They also evoke moral outrage because what the Walther attempted to do destroys human dignity and should never be tolerated.

When We're Right, We're Right

Sometimes we are so certain of being right, we try to convert others to our point of view. In some cases, it is a moral *imperative* (command) to do so. For instance, not having the vote was so abhorrent to nineteenth-century suffragist Susan B. Anthony that she tirelessly tried to convert others to her viewpoint. Without advocates like her, and other feminists who followed in her footsteps, we would encounter much more sexism in the U.S. today.

When moral righteousness becomes too narrow-minded, however, it leads to self-righteousness—believing your truth is the only truth. Moreover, unfairly inflicting your moral beliefs on others cheats you of their viewpoints and robs them of moral autonomy. According to Lisa Newton, we must not confuse *liberty*—having the *right* to think what you think—with *validity*—believing that what you morally conclude is right.[6] Distinguishing between righteousness and self-righteousness can be difficult. But it is also essential, because righteousness allows us to take firm moral stands, while self-righteousness cuts off the dialogue that is necessary for discovering the truth.

Too Much Tolerance

Ironically, too much tolerance is as bad as too little. For behavior like torture, enslavement, and abuse are always wrong—and should never be tolerated. Furthermore, tolerance can lead to apathy and permissiveness—and moral decline.

During the 1970s and early 1980s, "values clarification" was a popular moral curriculum in American schools. This method helped students think about what they truly valued. Teachers never gave their own moral opinion so that the school could not be criticized for imposing only one particular moral standard. However, according to William Damon, author of *The Moral Child*, by being so neutral, "teachers erroneously gave the message that there is no such thing as right or wrong, good or evil."[7] Values clarification also failed to criticize values that are materialistic and selfish.

"If I'm not hurting anyone else, what does it matter what I do?" you might ask. If you live alone on an island, it probably doesn't. But as long as you interact with others, it does.

The problem with the leave-me-alone philosophy is that it sets up a double standard. The rule for one person is different from the rule for another person. Such differences erode the justice and fairness we all need in order to get along.

Jeremy usually paid to play golf. But on Mondays, when the golf course was closed, he sneaked in and played for free. "One person using a golf course is not doing any harm," he reasoned. The moral question isn't harm, it is fairness. We are expected to follow moral rules that are meant for everyone, and not relative to who we are or what our situation is. This ensures that each of us holds up our end of the moral bargain without according ourselves special privileges or making exceptions to moral law.

Both freedom of speech and of the press protect our right to express differences of opinion. The legal system guarantees a certain amount of tolerance for different moral behavior. But there are limits to tolerance.

Moral issues like the right to refuse medical treatment, abortion, gun ownership, the use of marijuana, and surrogate parenthood all continue to challenge our tolerance for moral differences. There is no end to moral challenge, is there?

9

TOUGH CHOICES

In Chicago, the infant son of Rudy Linares swallowed a yellow balloon and stopped breathing. Despite emergency surgery to remove the balloon, the infant remained in a coma, unable to breathe without a respirator. His brain was so damaged that doctors told Rudy his son would never improve.

For weeks, Rudy and his family kept watch over the infant. Finally, unable to bear the grief any longer and convinced his son should die a natural death, Rudy pleaded with the hospital to disconnect the life support and let his son die. The hospital refused.

He sought help through the courts. But since his son, Sammy, still showed brain waves and therefore wasn't brain dead, the judges ruled to keep the baby on life support.

Rudy and his wife continued to visit Sammy. Often, Rudy came in the middle of the night. Holding his son in his arms, he would beg him to die.

Nine months after the accident, with no change in his son's condition or hope of improvement, Rudy decided his only choice was to take the situation into his own hands.

Armed with a gun to dissuade anyone from stopping him, Rudy unplugged his son's respirator. In response, the nurse on duty called security. As eight police officers watched, Rudy cradled his child in his arms while the infant peacefully died.

Rudy was arrested and hauled off to jail to face first-degree murder charges. A day after the arrest, he was surrounded by defense attorneys, eager to help.

Why did he risk twenty years in jail or even the electric chair? "I did what I had to do," explained Rudy. "I did it because I loved my son."[1]

According to Cook County medical examiner Dr. Robert Stein, who testified at the grand jury hearing, Sammy Linares had actually died at the time of the accident. When the grand jury refused to indict Linares on murder charges, the attorney who defended Rudy called it "compassionate justice."

Moral situations requiring difficult choices are called moral dilemmas. Moral dilemmas like Rudy's are complicated because the choices are never altogether good or bad. Neither of Rudy's two choices—to unhook his son's respirator himself or let his son live as a vegetable—was good. His decision to unhook the respirator was the best he could decide, and simply the "lesser of two evils."

As we have learned earlier, unless people are free to choose or to act, they cannot be held morally responsible for what they do. But the choices between right and wrong are not always clear-cut or easy to make. And like Rudy's choices, they can even be awful.

In a moral dilemma, the "right" choice may actually be "wrong" but merely the "best" choice under the circumstances. Being wrong, in fact, makes "best" difficult to determine.

For example, when terrorists hold innocent hostages, what is the duty of the hostages' government? One choice is to negotiate with the terrorists for the hostages' release. But this paves the way for continued terrorism and the taking of more hostages. Another choice is to refuse to negotiate at all. This discourages terrorism but can cost innocent hostages their lives. A third choice is to rescue the hostages. Again, as a bungled attempt—in which military personnel were killed—to rescue American hostages in Iran in 1980 proved, this too is risky and sometimes leads to tragic results.

In the mid-1960s, medical technology ushered in unprecedented lifesaving techniques. By then, kidney failure, a once fatal condition, could finally be treated with hemodialysis. But there weren't enough dialysis machines for all those who needed them. When a committee in Seattle, Washington, was discovered using criteria that included favoring married over single people, pillars of the community over prostitutes, and men over women, the moral debate over allocating scarce medical resources began.[2] And it has never ended.

Each day in the United States, one hundred babies die because the demand for newborn heart donors exceeds their supply.[3] Determining who will receive a transplant is an ethical decision—for the hospital, the doctors, the family of the deceased, and the family of the potential recipient. And it raises different issues for each of them. Moreover, any joy over receiving a new heart is shadowed by the anguish of the donor's death, and the awareness of the babies on the waiting list who are denied the heart they need in order to survive.

Following Your Conscience

Nearly all college students *say* that cheating is immoral. Yet when researchers Edward Diener and Mark Wollbom left college students alone to work on word problems, they observed a considerable distance between word and deed. Students who were left to work in front of a mirror and asked to listen to a tape-recorded voice were self-conscious enough to keep to their word—only 7 percent cheated. When left completely alone, however, nearly three out of four students cheated by working past the bell.[4]

Adults act similarly. In a National Opinion Research Survey of adult Americans, 75 percent said stealing is wrong, yet most of them admitted they would steal anyway. And a May 17, 1988, *New York Times* survey reported that, on the average, adults admitted to lying *thirteen* times a week.[5]

There are many reasons why we don't follow our conscience or do the right thing. Torn between loyalty to our friends, family, employees, or the government, or caught in our own ambivalence about what is right or wrong, we often ignore our conscience. Explaining the reason why he participated in the famous Watergate break-in of the Democratic party's national headquarters, and later in a cover-up, Jeb Magruder, President Richard Nixon's public relations spokesman, said, "I ignored my conscience because my loyalty to the President was greater."[6]

Moral *dilemmas* entail a struggle to decide what is best. In contrast, moral *conflict* occurs when you know what is best, but you struggle over doing it.

In a free society, we have the individual right to disagree, protest, or disobey anything that goes against our conscience and against what we think is right. That can take considerable courage and conviction, sometimes more than most of us are willing or able to muster.

People in authority are constantly teaching us to respect and obey them. They often give us good advice. But when you're used to respecting and obeying authority, it is difficult to challenge that authority, as Stanley Milgram's experiment proved, even when your conscience tells you to do so.

Among friends, family, or colleagues, taking a stand can be socially awkward. For example, racist jokes are wrong. They hurt people's feelings and reinforce negative stereotypes. At a family gathering, your grandfather is regaling the company with a racist joke. Telling him that he is wrong and that you are offended, especially if he is sensitive and caring toward you and your family, is very awkward and difficult.

When the Going Gets Tough

If moral decisions involve a great risk or sacrifice, they cause a lot of conflict. They should.

For instance, should a breadwinner risk unemployment to take a stand against a supervisor he or she knows is stealing company stationery or office supplies? Or should a person risk his or her life to save an animal in danger?

When Socrates chose to die for his principles, his friend Crito asked him, while there was still time to change his sentence or to escape, to consider the effect Socrates' death would have on his two young sons.[7]

Socrates refused to compromise, even for the sake of his sons. Although dying was a terrible price to pay for taking a stand, Socrates felt he would pay a greater price if he compromised his values and gave in to the state or fled from Athens. He believed that he would never again be the same person he had been. And for Socrates, that was a fate worse than death.

In a different vein, William Bennett, former director of federal drug policy, suggested that turning in a friend who uses drugs is an "act of true loyalty, not snitching or betrayal."

According to one student from a tough Chicago neighborhood, turning in a friend may be loyal, but it is also too dangerous. "If I squeal on a friend . . .

my friend won't be my friend no more. . . . And maybe I won't be no more. There are people around here, if they find out I told on one of them, they might put me away for good. Maybe in some fancy suburb they can do that stuff, but in those suburbs, kids don't pack a piece or a knife."[8]

Excuses, Excuses

On the night of March 13, 1964, Kitty Genovese, a young woman, was assaulted on her way home.[9] After the brutal stabbing, she pleaded for help, screaming, "Oh, my God, he stabbed me! Please help me? Please help me!"

It was three A.M. in her Queens, New York, neighborhood. Most people were asleep. Yet Kitty's screams attracted the attention of thirty-eight bystanders. From an open window, one person shouted to her attacker, "Let that girl alone!"

But no one came to Kitty's aid, even after her attacker disappeared. Not a single person telephoned the police.

Kitty struggled to her feet and staggered down the street, and around the corner toward her apartment building.

Then, to her horror, the man who stabbed her reappeared—and stabbed her again. "I'm dying," she cried out, "I'm dying."

The attacker left, got into his car, and drove off.

Kitty collapsed. This time, she crawled slowly toward her building. She got as far as her doorway when the attacker appeared once more, to stab her a third time. Then he vanished into the night.

More than forty minutes after the first attack, only one person helped—by calling the police. Within two minutes, the police arrived. But by now, Kitty Genovese had died.

Her assailant, Winston Mosely, a twenty-nine-year-old business machine operator, was apprehended and later convicted.

Bystanders have no moral commitment to risk their lives to rescue someone else. But certainly, calling the police in the security of your own home should cause no moral conflict. Fear and moral conflict often paralyze people into doing nothing. But neither apathy nor indifference, both expressions of not caring, are adequate excuses. "The only thing necessary for the triumph of evil," to quote eighteenth-century philosopher Edmund Burke, "is for good men to do nothing."[10]

These examples are not meant to dissuade you from behaving morally when doing so requires great sacrifice. Rather, they are meant to help you become more sensitive to real moral conflict. For it is easy to discuss a hypothetical situation and *say* that we will never follow orders that go against our conscience, or never get duped or bribed into going against our good judgment.

Observing the people who *do* follow their conscience, the mother of Ruby Bridges, one of the young black children who bravely confronted threats and jeers to desegregate her elementary school in New Orleans, said: "There are a lot of people who always worry about whether they're doing right or doing wrong. But there are some other folks who just put their lives on the line for what's right and they may not be the ones who talk a lot or argue a lot or worry a lot; they just *do* a lot!"[11]

Which End Is Up?

Being sure of what to do in a moral situation is called moral certainty. The opposite is moral uncertainty or moral ambiguity. People who possess clear-cut, absolute principles are usually morally certain about what is right. (They are not necessarily *right*, they are only *certain* about being right.)

Two separate studies showed that a strict religious upbringing substantially contributes to a person's moral certainty.[12] One reason is that many religions teach straightforward definitions of right and wrong and good and bad.

In one survey of young people, researchers found that much moral uncertainty was tied to affluence. Children who live in the wealthiest communities (where the median income is forty thousand dollars per year) are most likely to be morally indecisive when asked questions like:

"If you were presented with a drink at a party, what would you do?"
"If you found out your friend was pregnant, what would you advise her?"

"How would you respond to knowledge that a close friend was homosexual?"[13]

Often, morally indecisive children answered, "I don't know."

Researchers speculated that one reason for such ambiguity was that growing up with wealth and education offers a wider range of options and choices. And apparently, it is more difficult to narrow down so many options.

Making difficult moral decisions is mentally taxing and often heartbreaking. Pressed for time, we may fail to acquire all of the information we need to make an informed decision. Or time may be too brief to weigh all of the choices and consider all of the consequences. Duress and fear may strain our ability to think clearly. As one woman explained of her decision to have an abortion, which she later regretted: "I found out I was pregnant on a Saturday afternoon and had the abortion the following Tuesday morning. Who can make an important decision rationally like that in two days?"[14]

Decision-making often involves uncertainty, especially when we make decisions under difficult circumstances. Even when the outcome is tragic, many people take solace in believing that they did the best they could at the time.

In another "voice" from the abortion issue, a father said of the decision that he and his wife made to abort their Down's syndrome fetus, "I have never felt such grief and sorrow . . . never had to face a choice so difficult."[15] Although he felt terrible about having to make the decision at all, he said he had no regrets about it.

Many people are encumbered not only by doubt but also by guilt over decisions they later regret. With the wisdom of hindsight, they continue to play the decision over and over in their heads. "If only I had known then what I know now, if only I had acted differently." "If only" plagues them long after the decision has been made.

Some people, in fact, are so morally uncertain, so fearful of making a wrong decision, that they are unable to make any moral decision at all. Instead, they defer to others, not only for advice and direction but to actually make their moral decisions for them, and perhaps even to take moral action as well. Others rely on the flip of the coin or their horoscope to tell them what to do. Still others procrastinate—putting off their decision until they are *reacting* to a situation instead of acting on it. Yet *not* making a decision is actually making a decision itself.

When you are faced with a moral dilemma or conflict, it helps to seek advice from people whose opinions you respect. Sometimes just talking about your situation gives you a better perspective on it. Parents, teachers, trusted friends, counselors, clergy, or other moral advisers can point out choices you overlooked, discuss consequences you neglected to consider, and explore creative ways of taking action you hadn't imagined. In addition, they give you moral support and confidence to take moral action.

The only way to be an autonomous individual, though, is to make your *own* moral decisions. These can—and should—be as informed, as principled, and as kind as possible. But to be moral, they must also be your own.

10

GETTING YOUR ACT TOGETHER

I am only one,
But still I am one.
I cannot do everything.
But still I can do something;
And because I cannot do everything
I will not refuse to do the something
that I can do.

—EDWARD EVERETT HALE[1]

If the South American rain forests continue disappearing at the current rate, in sixty years there will be nothing left of them.[2] Ben Cohen and John Reed worried about the rain forests and put their worry to work in moral action.

With a childhood friend, Ben Cohen had built a multimillion-dollar ice cream empire—Ben and Jerry's. After that accomplishment, Ben used his financial wizardry to start a new company, called Community Products, Inc. Among the items they market are a Brazil nut-and-cashew candy and Rainforest Crunch Cookies. As their chief ingredient both products use the Brazil nut that grows wild in the Amazon and is harvested by local people who live off the rain forest without destroying it. "Just by buying and eating Rainforest Crunch Cookies," Ben tells customers, "you help save the rain forest."[3] Because he was already wealthy from his ice cream business, Ben's new company was not a huge gamble or financial sacrifice. In fact, he commits 60 percent of its profits to peace and environmental concerns.

In contrast, when Clevelander John Reed refrained from stocking his furniture stores with any products made from teak, Brazilian mahogany, or any other tropical rain forest wood, he lost as much as three hundred thousand dollars a year in sales.[4] "I've thought about this problem for many months," Reed explained of his action, "and I took a stand."

Alone, neither Ben Cohen nor John Reed can stop the destruction of the rain forests. "My move may seem insignificant," Reed says. Still, their moral standards inspire them to tackle the problem anyway. For to paraphrase Edward Everett Hale's earlier quote, "Nobody made a greater mistake than he who did nothing because he could only do a little."

As we have learned throughout this book, ethics usually involves struggle—determining what to do—then *doing* it. For many reasons, from laziness and indifference to uncertainty and fear, we sometimes fail to take moral action—as individuals, communities, or nations.

What does it take to get our moral act together? Indeed, does it matter if we do—or don't?

What's in It for Me?

"What's in it for me?" is a natural question. Some ethicists believe that moral action is really "enlightened self-interest." They think people don't do anything moral unless there is something in it for them, if only the self-respect that comes from acting right and doing good.

But Michael Schulman and Eva Mekler, authors of *Bringing Up a Moral Child*, suggest that there are several kinds of practical, emotional, and spiritual rewards for moral living.[5]

Because it makes sense. Schulman and Mekler write that as long as we need other people for "aid, comfort, and ordinary necessities," it is practical to treat them fairly and kindly. Although exceptions arise, in general others are inclined to treat us as we treat them, a twist on the Golden Rule: "Others do unto you as you do unto them." Treat them badly and it will boomerang right back to you. Treat them well and they'll probably treat you well in return.

Another practical reason for acting morally is that you are most likely to stay out of trouble! Immoral behavior often leads to trouble and punishment, especially when you break the law.

Because it feels good. As we learned in chapter three, when we do good for others, we feel good about it. In this way, moral action gives us strong emotional rewards. Doing good for someone else is, in fact, one of the best antidotes when you are feeling sorry for yourself.

By acting morally, you also benefit from having a "clear conscience," and the feeling of pride, security, and self-respect that goes along with that.

Just because. The most important reason for moral living is to build a better world. "Doing good adds more love, justice and caring to the world, and less fear, pain and suffering," claim Schulman and Mekler, "and ultimately, *when you strive for moral living, you are leading the best life a human being can lead.*"[6] This is something you have to experience for yourself in order to appreciate.

Making a Difference

> If everyone did their share,
> no one would have to save the entire world.
> —TWELVE-YEAR-OLD FROM OHIO

It's easy to think that someone else's problems aren't our responsibility. One person can't save the entire world, we reason. Or, if we think we are already carrying our share of the load (and maybe we are), why not wait for others to take on their share?

When we see goodness that goes unrewarded and crime that seems to pay, it's natural to ask: Why be good (especially when no one else is)?

It's tempting to lower our moral standards. Occasionally, going against them is even exciting.

Nobody's perfect, we tell ourselves. Besides, in the

whole scheme of things, what difference does it make—for better or worse?

For most ordinary moral behavior like returning change when you have been undercharged on a restaurant bill, the difference we make is difficult to measure. What counts, however, is not *how much* of a difference your moral behavior makes, but that it makes *any difference at all*.

In Poland, during World War II, Anna Polhalski dug a hole under her bedroom floor. In that tiny hole, a young Jewish boy named Felix Zandman, his uncle, and a Jewish couple hid from the Nazis for five hundred days. And although they didn't hide in her bedroom refuge, Anna also helped rescue three other Jews from the Nazis, who would have killed them—and Anna and her five children for helping them.[7]

By 1990, these seven survivors, together with their children and grandchildren, numbered forty-five. Forty-five people would not have been alive forty-five years after the war were it not for the moral commitment and action of one courageous woman—Anna Polhalski (a "righteous Gentile," as she and others like her are affectionately called by Jewish survivors).

Between 1940 and 1944, the inhabitants of a French village, le Chambon-sur-Lignon, showed what happens when the moral courage of individuals comes together. From his pulpit, Pastor Trocmé, the moral leader of his community, taught that if each person lived by the commandment to love one's neighbor as oneself, he or she could withstand the forces of evil. "We do not know what a Jew is," he told the officers who asked him where Jews were hiding. "We only know men."[8]

Right under the noses of the Vichy government, which collaborated with the Nazis, and later of the Gestapo, Le Chambon's residents refused to cooperate with Nazi officials by hiding Jews and helping them reach safety. Together, the small village of less than four thousand saved twenty-five hundred Jews from death.[9]

You don't always need courage to save another person's life. Sometimes moral commitment and caring suffice.

Every day, forty thousand children in the world die of preventable causes—starvation, disease, illness, and war.[10] On September 29, 1990, a World Summit for Children convened at the United Nations to focus awareness on the plight of these children. Through media programs and articles, the information that a simple ten-dollar donation could save the life of a child for one year reached millions of people. By donating money to a joint program between Save the Children and UNICEF, ordinary people could save children's lives. And indeed they did. Nine-year-old Dave Jordan gave ten dollars to save one child. And together, thousands of Americans donated millions of dollars to save hundreds of thousands of children's lives.

Saving a life is one of the most noble moral acts we can do. But every time we pay someone an honest compliment, return a lost object, take a test honestly, refrain from hurting someone, or right a wrong, we make a moral difference. Collectively, these actions add up to big differences.

Sometimes what one person does seems insignificant—until his or her moral action snowballs into something grand.

When Wendy Kopp attended a conference addressing the sorry state of American education, she thought of a unique solution to the problem—a Teacher's Corps like the Peace Corps, with teachers recruited from the ranks of graduating college students.[11] During her senior year at Princeton University, Wendy turned her idea into a senior thesis, then into a corporate proposal requesting grants to fund the corps.

By the end of the summer after her graduation, Wendy had persuaded major corporations like Mobil and Xerox to donate more than $1 million. She had also hired twenty-three college graduates to staff the program, worked with the University of Southern California and the Los Angeles Department of Education to establish an eight-week crash course to train the graduates as teachers, recruited two thousand five hundred eager applicants (which was narrowed down to a select five hundred), and found rural and inner-city schools desperately in need of the teachers her corps would provide.

Just as moral action can make a positive difference, immoral action also makes a difference—for the worse.

Taking a pencil here and a notepad there

shouldn't do much damage to a company's overall budget. But according to the Fireman's Fund Insurance Company, at least $67 *billion* are lost each year in the United States to employee cheating and stealing.[12] This includes everything from padding expense accounts to pilfering office supplies.

Like the office workers who think their little "misdemeanors" make little difference, Kimberlee Lewen thought nothing of stealing a cheap bottle of wine one night.[13] When a clerk who spotted the theft reported it, police arrested the twenty-four-year-old Lewen. Because she had been arrested twice before for stealing, the judge set her bail at ten thousand dollars and charged her with felony. As a result, Lewen spent over two months in jail.

How much damage could a few dollars' theft have done? Said Medina, Ohio, county sheriff L. John Ribar, "I know she thinks it was just one bottle, but if five hundred people thought that, it would drive someone out of business."[14]

Protecting against theft puts quite a burden on businesses' budgets—to the tune of billions of dollars each year. Nor is business the only victim of crime. According to the U.S. Department of Justice, each year since 1982, one out of every four American households—nearly 23 million—has been victimized by a crime of violence or theft.[15]

Often we are unaware of the difference our actions make. Though it pales in comparison to the oil slick that occurred during the Persian Gulf War and that extended for miles and did untold damage, pouring just a pint of used automobile oil into the street or sewer can eventually create an oil slick an acre in diameter.[16]

And, finally, whether it's graffiti on a bathroom stall, vandalism in a park, or international terrorism, one misdeed frequently paves the way for more.

Getting Your Moral Act Together

For thousands of years, families, religions, and various philosophies have tried to show us how to live morally. They give us simple principles and complex moral theories. They give us biblical prescriptions, humanist traditions, and professional codes. They give us heroes and heroines to inspire us, laws to guide us, and courts to chide us. Yet living morally remains an awesome challenge.

Moral dilemmas and conflicts have neither clearcut solutions nor easy answers. With our personal shortcomings, we struggle to act good and be good. And sometimes we give up the struggle. It's enough to make the wisest philosopher, kindest theologian, and most perceptive psychologist scurry away in search of a magic formula for moral living.

The purpose of this book is not to give you easy answers either, but to encourage you to find your own moral code. Following are just a few general guidelines to help you.

Wake-up. The first step is waking up to ethics. Learn which moral issues need your attention—and action.

Remember both the importance of moral conviction and the humbleness of moral uncertainty, of when to tolerate and when to be intolerant.

Think before you act. Moral decisions require that we weigh as much information as we can gather, listen to *all* sides of an issue, and consider the interests of everyone involved. You also need to consider the effect of your decisions, not only now, but in the future—months, years, and, according to the advice of the Great Law of the Hau de no saunee Indians, even seven generations from now.

Making wise decisions means thinking before you speak, but thinking twice before you act—when time permits. When it doesn't, follow your heart. As we have learned, ethics is more than a way of thinking—it is also a way of feeling. So when you feel something is right, go for it.

Do the right thing. Every day presents opportunities to act morally. Look for them. Or when they "find you," embrace them—as challenges, opportunities for growth, and tests of moral courage. This means overcoming laziness, indifference, fear, and temptation, no small order for even the saints among us. And most of all, it means doing the right thing.

When you walk through a storm. It is easy to be good when the stakes are low and the rewards are high. But as Martin Luther King, Jr., said, a person's worth is "not where he stands in moments of comfort and convenience, but where he stands at times of challenge and controversy."[17]

When you face tough moral decisions or difficult situations, remember to hold fast to your principles, follow your moral compass, and cultivate the courage required of you. Keep your moral imagination and vision of a better tomorrow active.

Be kind to yourself. In ethics, striving to be a virtuous person is a worthwhile goal. But like most difficult goals, it is easy to miss the mark.

Getting your act together *some*times doesn't mean you have it together *all* the time. Nobody does. Our greatest moral heroes and heroines have human foibles and personal shortcomings. Rabbi Shlomo Carlebach of New York advises that we strive for goodness and set realistic goals. "Don't try to be *very* good every day," he says. "Instead try each day to do a *little* something good."[18]

Just as Rabbi Carlebach advises us to be realistic in our moral expectations, we can also reach for what appears unreachable, attain what appears unattainable, and make our moral mark on the world. After all, if you reach *all* of your goals, you haven't set them high enough.

ENDNOTES

Chapter 1

1. "Miller Proves Honesty's Best," *Hudson Hub-Times*, Hudson, Ohio (September 25, 1990).
2. Many states have laws against finders keepers. In California, for example, it is a felony to keep anything more valuable than four hundred dollars.
3. "How Honest Are You?" *20/20* (aired June 9, 1989).
4. Ezra Bowen, "What Ever Became of Honest Abe?" *Time* (April 5, 1988):68.
5. Samantha Smith, *Journey to the Soviet Union* (Boston: Little, Brown & Co., 1984).
6. Viktor Frankl, *Man's Search for Meaning* (New York: Washington Square Press, 1984), p. 12.
7. Mary Mahowald, personal interview (October 29, 1990).
8. Robert Lawry, "Ethics, Character and the Professions," *Center for Professional Ethics of Case Western Reserve University*, newsletter (Fall 1987):1, 5.
9. William Schmidt, "Treating Adultery as Crime: Wisconsin Dusts Off Old Law," *New York Times* (April 30, 1990).
10. Arthur Dobrin, *The God Within* (New York: Ethica Press, 1977), p. 11.
11. Ibid., p. 19.
12. Susan Rasky, "The Entire Senate Is About to Have

Ethics Problems," *New York Times* (December 31, 1989).

Chapter 2

1. Trish Hall, "How Classroom Crusaders Saved the Dolphin From the Net," *New York Times* (April 18, 1990).
2. John Robbins, *Diet for a New America* (Walpole, N.H.: Stillpoint Publishing, 1987), p. 31.
3. Quoted in Molly O'Neill, "Will Too Many Sentiments Spoil the Cook?" *New York Times* (August 8, 1990).
4. Producing one pound of steak uses 2500 gallons of water; from Frances Moore Lappé, *Diet for a Small Planet* (New York: Ballantine Books, 1982), p. 10.
5. Ibid., p. 76.
6. Dirk Johnson, "Ryan White Dies of AIDS at 18: His Struggle Helps Pierce Myths," *New York Times* (April 9, 1990).
7. The model for moral imagination comes from Michael Schulman and Eva Mekler, *Bringing Up a Moral Child* (New York: Addison-Wesley, 1985), pp. 90–1.
8. William Robbins, "Acts of Charity Spring from Rock of Honesty," *New York Times* (December 16, 1990).
9. "The Ferrell Family's Unlikely Crusade," *McCall's* (January 1985):54.
10. "Trevor Ferrell," Giraffe Project Middle School Curriculum, Student Activities (January 1981). For more information, write: Trevor's Campaign for the Homeless, 137-139 E. Spring Ave., Ardmore, PA 19003.

Chapter 3

1. "Drum Major Instinct" sermon given at Ebenezer Baptist Church, Atlanta, Georgia (February 4, 1968).
2. "American Heroes of '88," *Geraldo* transcript (aired December 14, 1988):7.
3. Douglas Martin, "A Beauty Parlor That Tries to Restore Dignity as Well," *New York Times* (April 25, 1990).
4. Schulman and Mekler, *Bringing Up a Moral Child*, p. 15.
5. Morton Hunt, *The Compassionate Beast* (New York: William Morrow, 1990), p. 105.
6. Schulman and Mekler, *Bringing Up a Moral Child*, pp. 12–13.
7. Lawrence Kohlberg, *The Philosophy of Moral Development*, vol. 1 (San Francisco: Harper & Row, Publ., 1981), p. 12.
8. Paraphrased from responses to capital punishment. *Ibid*, pp. 260–5.
9. Quoted in Thomas Likona, ed., *Moral Behavior and Development: Theory, Research, and Social Issues* (New York: Holt, Rinehart and Winston, 1975), chapter 2; cited in Schulman and Mekler, *Bringing Up a Moral Child*, p. 15.
10. "The Cast of Characters," *The Giraffe Gazette*, newsletter, (Summer 1990):11.
11. "The Cast of Characters," p. 10.
12. Carol Gilligan, preface, *Mapping the Moral Domain*, ed. Carol Gilligan et al. (Cambridge, Mass.: Harvard University Press, 1982), p. ix.
13. Hunt, *The Compassionate Beast*, p. 105.
14. William Damon, *The Moral Child* (New York: Free Press, 1989), p. 15.

15. Ibid.
16. Ibid.
17. Ibid.
18. Ibid., p. 17.
19. M. Toi and C. D. Batson, *Journal of Personality and Social Psychology* 43 (1982):281–92; cited in Schulman and Mekler, *Bringing Up a Moral Child*, p. 51.
20. *The Chance of a Lifetime: Questions and Answers about Marrow Transplants*, pamphlet (National Marrow Donor Program), p. 11.
21. Ibid.
22. *Carnegie Hero Fund Commission 1989 Annual Report*, booklet (Pittsburgh: Carnegie Fund, 1990), p. 14.
23. Quoted in Carol Gilligan, "Remapping the Moral Domain," in ed. Gilligan et al., *Mapping the Moral Domain*, p. 14.
24. Martin Luther King, Jr., *Strength to Love* (Philadelphia: Fortress Press, 1985), p. 10.
25. Quoted in Schulman and Mekler, *Bringing Up a Moral Child*, p. 15.

Chapter 4

1. Frank Trippett, "Guilty, Guilty, Guilty," *Time* (August 27, 1990):40.
2. Fox Butterfield, "The Uproar at Dartmouth: How a Conservative Weekly Inflamed a Campus," *New York Times* (October 6, 1990).
3. James Patterson and Peter Kim, *The Day America Told the Truth* (New York: Prentice Hall, 1991), p. 45.
4. National Institute on Drug Abuse, *National House-*

hold Survey on Drug Abuse: Main Findings 1985 (Washington, D.C.: U.S. Department of Health and Human Services, 1988), p. 16.

5. All three examples are from *The Giraffe Gazette,* newsletter (Summer 1990):10–11.

6. Barbara Dafoe Whitehead, "Children in an Amoral Culture," *Cleveland Plain Dealer* (October 22, 1990).

7. Damon, *The Moral Child,* p. xiv; and Schulman and Mekler, *Bringing Up a Moral Child,* p. 4.

8. Samuel and Pearl Oliner, *The Altruistic Personality* (New York: Free Press, 1988).

9. *Girl Scout Survey of Children's Moral Beliefs and Values* (New York: Girl Scouts of America, 1990), pp. 2, 6.

10. Ignacio L. Gotz, "Is There a Moral Skill?" *Educational Theory* (Winter 1989):11.

11. Alice Miller, *For Your Own Good,* 3d ed., translated by Hildegarde and Hunter Hannum (New York: Farrar, Straus and Giroux, 1990), pp. 83–4.

12. Lisa Newton, ed., *Ethics in America: Source Reader* (Englewood Cliffs, N.J.: Prentice Hall, 1989), pp. 66–7.

13. Wade Clark Roof and David A. Roozen, who conducted a study of Lily Foundation; cited in Kenneth Woodward et al., "And the Children Shall Lead Them," *Newsweek* (December 17, 1990):50.

14. *Girl Scout Survey,* p. 2.

15. Robert Coles, *The Spiritual Life of Children* (Boston: Houghton Mifflin, 1990), pp. 2–3.

16. Min Yee and Thomas Layton, *In My Father's House* (New York: Holt, Rinehart and Winston, 1981), p. 310.

17. "Ethical Culture Society," *Encyclopedia Britannica,* vol. 3, 15th ed. (1982):976.

18. Damon, *The Moral Child,* p. 146.
19. Eleanor Blau, "From Moral Tracts to Tom Thumbe," *New York Times* (December 5, 1990).
20. Benjamin Franklin, *Poor Richard's Almanack* (Mount Vernon, N.Y.: Peter Pauper Press).
21. *McCollum* v. *Bd. of Education,* 333 U.S. 203 (1948).
22. *Zorach* v. *Clausen,* 343 U.S. 306 (1952).
23. *Engle* v.*Vitale,* 370 U.S. 421 (1962).
24. *Abington School District* v. *Schempp; Murray* v. *Curlett,* 374 U.S. 203 (1963).
25. Edmund Lindop, *The Bill of Rights and Landmark Cases* (New York: Franklin Watts, 1989), p. 49.
26. Alex M. Gallup and David L. Clark, "The 19th American Gallup Poll of Public's Attitudes Toward the Public Schools," *Phi Delta Kappan* (September 1987):24.
27. *Religion in the Public School Curriculum— Questions and Answers,* pamphlet.
28. Ibid.
29. *Report of the Advisory Council on Developing Character and Values in New Jersey Students* Trenton, N.J.): State Board of Education, March 1989), p. 7.
30. Fred Hechinger, "About Education: Community Service Work," *New York Times* (July 4, 1990).
31. Lisa W. Foderaro, "At Rye High, Students Not Only Must Do Well, They Must Do Good," *New York Times* (April 30, 1990).
32. Damon, *The Moral Child,* p. 152.
33. Quoted in P. K. Saka, "English Professor, Case Western Reserve University," *Northern Ohio Live Magazine* (February 1983), p. 24.
34. Miller, *For Your Own Good,* p. 105.

Chapter 5

1. Michael Sokolove, *Hustling: The Myth, Life and Lies of Pete Rose* (New York: Simon & Schuster, 1990), p. 14.
2. Rose can apply for reinstatement after one year, but of the fourteen players who previously were suspended, none had ever been reinstated. Ibid., p. 277.
3. Claire Smith, "Rose Sentenced to 5 Months For Filing False Tax Returns," *New York Times* (July 20, 1990).
4. Quoted by Peter Pascarelli, *The National* (February 21, 1990); cited in Sokolove, *Hustling*, p. 285.
5. Excerpted from statement Rose made at his sentencing in Court, reprinted in "I Really Have No Excuses," *New York Times* (July 20, 1990).
6. Murray Chass, "Hall of Fame Panel Moves to Keep Pete Rose Out," *New York Times* (January 11, 1991).
7. Chuck Philips, "Milli Vanilli Duo Repent and Beg for Forgiveness," *Cleveland Plain Dealer* (November 24, 1990); and Jon Pareles, "Wages of Silence: Milli Vanilli Loses Its Grammy Award," *New York Times* (November 20, 1990).
8. Jon Pareles, "Should Milli Vanilli Take the Rap for the Industry?" *New York Times* (December 2, 1990).
9. Stephen Bodian, "Love Is the Healer: An Interview with Joan Borysenko," *Yoga Journal* (May/June 1990):98.
10. Quoted in Bodian, "Love Is the Healer," p. 48.
11. Alan Miller, "Repentant Thief Returns Loot," *Columbus Dispatch*, Columbus, Ohio (January 22, 1989).

12. "Amazing Grace with Bill Moyers," transcript (aired September 12, 1990).

13. Ibid., p. 17.

14. "Lying, Cheating, Stealing in America," transcript, *Burning Questions* (aired June 1, 1989):11.

15. Patterson and Kim, *The Day America Told the Truth*, p. 236.

Chapter 6

1. *New York Times* (November 25, 1969); cited in Schulman and Mekler, *Bringing Up a Moral Child*, p. 109.

2. Seymour Hersh, *Cover-up* (New York: Random House, 1972), p. 7.

3. Stanley Milgram, *Obedience to Authority* (New York: Harper & Row, Publ., 1974), p. 185.

4. Ibid.

5. C. P. Snow, "Either-Or," *The Progressive* (February 1961):24; cited in Milgram, *Obedience to Authority*, p. 2.

6. Ibid., pp. 4, 215.

7. Milgram, *Obedience to Authority*, p. 2.

8. Lena Williams, "Teenage Sex: New Codes Amid the Old Anxiety," *New York Times* (February 27, 1989).

9. Mark Hoffman, ed., *World Almanac*, (New York: Pharos Books, 1990), p. 824.

10. Any state can require a minor who is not emancipated (living on her own) to obtain either parental consent or judicial determination (a judge's consent to make the decision herself). *Parental Notice Laws*, pamphlet (New York: Reproductive Freedom Project of the American Civil Liberties Union, 1986):18–19.

11. Personal interview with author; name has been changed (July 1986).
12. Milgram, *Obedience to Authority*, p. 2.
13. Ibid., p. 8.

Chapter 7

1. Coles, *The Spiritual Life of Children*, p. 25.
2. Judith Jarvis Thomson, *Rights, Restitution, & Risk* (Cambridge, Mass.: Harvard University Press), p. 255.
3. "Milken Sentenced to 10 Years in Prison," *Cleveland Plain Dealer* (November 22, 1990).
4. Larry Reibstein, "Throwing the Book at Milken," *Newsweek* (December 3, 1990):42.
5. Kurt Eichenwald, "Term is Longest of Any Given in Scandal," *New York Times* (November 22, 1990).
6. Newton, ed., *Ethics in America: Source Reader*, p. 191.
7. Lisa Newton, ed., *Ethics in America: Study Guide* (Englewood Cliffs, N.J.: Prentice Hall, 1989), p. 31.
8. Reverend Read Heydt, personal interview (January 30, 1991).
9. Philip Shenon, "A H.U.D. Agent Details Taking $5 Million," *New York Times* (June 11, 1989).
10. Gloria Steinem, "Is a Feminist Ethic the Answer?" *Ms.* (September 1987):62.
11. Frankl, *Man's Search for Meaning*, p. 17.
12. Martin Luther King, Jr., *Why We Can't Wait* (New York: Harper & Row, Publ., 1963, pp. 76–95.
13. Ibid.
14. Michael Josephson, "The IDIs Are Coming! The IDIs Are Coming!" *Ethics: Easier Said than Done* (October 1990):34.

15. Newton, *Ethics in America*, Study Guide, p. 34.
16. Ibid.
17. From the Gospel According to Luke, 10:25; cited in Newton, *Source Book*, p. 86.
18. Cited in Robert Schnell and Elizabeth Hall, *Developmental Psychology Today*, 4th ed. (New York: Random House, 1983), p. 393.
19. Quoted in Tom Huth, "You're a Dirty Rotten Liar . . . ," *California* (October 1990):84.
20. As a group, clergy earn much respect for their profession. In 1985, 67 percent of those interviewed thought clergy had high or very high ethical standards; but by 1990, only 55 percent of respondents gave them such a good rating. Graham Hueber, "Pharmacists and Clergy Again Rated Highest for Honesty and Ethical Standards," *Gallup Poll News Service* (February 28, 1990).
21. "Mayor's Wife Quiet About His Affair," *Cleveland Plain Dealer* (November 22, 1990).
22. Paraphrased from Samuel and Pearl Oliner, *The Altruistic Personality*, p. 249.

Chapter 8

1. "Power to Heal: Medical Ethics and Religious Freedom," *Nightline* (aired September 22, 1983):2.
2. Ibid., p. 6.
3. Lisa Newton, ed., *Ethics in America: Study Guide*, pp. 16–17.
4. Susan Terkel, *Should Drugs Be Legalized?* (New York: Franklin Watts, 1990), p. 15.
5. "Estranged Couple Strapped by Bills Offers to Sell a Son," *Cleveland Plain Dealer* (October 10, 1990).

6. Newton, *Ethics in America: Study Guide*, pp. 16–17.
7. Damon, *The Moral Child*, pp. 133–4.

Chapter 9

1. "A Father's Desperate Act," *20/20* (aired December 8, 1989):2–8; Society for the Right to Die, letter (1990); Alex J. Koleszar, "The Great Debate," *Center for Professional Ethics of Case Western Reserve University*, newsletter (February 1990):16.
2. Katherine Bouton, "Painful Decisions: The Role of the Medical Ethicist," *New York Times Magazine* (August 5, 1990): 25.
3. Quoted by Dr. Bailey in "Serious Heart Defect Heals, Amazing Doctors," *New York Times* (October 9, 1990).
4. David Myers, *Social Psychology*, 2d ed. (New York: McGraw-Hill, 1987), p. 44.
5. *Take an Honest Look*, pamphlet (Columbus, Ohio: Columbus Commission on Ethics and Values, 1989).
6. "Magruder Dismisses Cynics," *Columbus Dispatch*, Columbus, Ohio (January 16, 1989).
7. Plato, *The Crito*, reprinted in Newton, *Source Reader*, pp. 14–17; discussed in I. F. Stone, *The Trial of Socrates* (Boston: Little, Brown & Co., 1988).
8. Quoted in Mike Royko's, "Many Would Tell on Drug-Using Pals," *Chicago Tribune* (June 12, 1989).
9. Leon Sheleff, *The Bystander* (Lexington, Mass.: Lexington Books, 1978), pp. 1–2; Hunt, *The Compassionate Beast*, pp. 128–9.
10. Quoted from "Thoughts on the Cause of the Present Discontents," essay, April 23, 1770; quoted in *Bart-*

lett's Familiar Quotations (New York: Random House, 1980), p. 372.

11. Quoted in Robert Coles, *The Moral Life of Children* (Boston: Houghton Mifflin, 1986), p. 22.

12. Gloria Steinem, "If Moral Decay Is the Question, Is a Feminist Ethic the Answer?" *Ms.* (September 1987):59; and *Girl Scout Survey on the Beliefs and Moral Values of American Children.*

13. *Girl Scout Survey*, pp. 53, 102.

14. Anonymous letter to Senator Gordon Humphrey; quoted in Terkel, *Abortion: Facing the Issues* (New York: Franklin Watts, 1988), p. 69.

15. Ibid., p. 88.

Chapter 10

1. Quoted in *Bartlett's Familiar Quotations*, p. 590.

2. Jerry Adler and Carolyn Friday, "Calories of the Rain Forest," *Newsweek* (December 3, 1990):61.

3. Ibid., p. 61.

4. Donald Sabath, "Rain Forests Have a Friend at Furniture Store Chain," *Cleveland Plain Dealer* (November 29, 1990).

5. Schulman and Mekler, *Bringing Up a Moral Child*, pp. 85–90.

6. Ibid.

7. "Thy Brothers' Keeper," *Sixty Minutes* (April 15, 1990):9–10.

8. Susan H. Kahn, "French Village Saving Others Also Saved Him, Says Author," *Cleveland Jewish News* (November 23, 1990):3.

9. Philip Hallie, *Lest Innocent Blood Be Shed* (New York: Harper & Row, Publ., 1979), p. 169.

10. Telephone interview, U.S. Committee for UNICEF (December 4, 1990).

11. Susan Chira, "Princeton Student's Brainstorm: A Peace Corps To Train Teachers," *New York Times* (June 20, 1990).

12. Reported by Bettina Gregory, "Lying, Cheating, Stealing in America," *Burning Questions* (June 8, 1989):13.

13. Michael Sangiacomo, "A Long Time for Wine," *Cleveland Plain Dealer* (December 19, 1990).

14. Ibid.

15. Michael R. Rand, "Crime and the Nation's Households, 1989," bulletin (U.S. Department of Justice, Bureau of Justice Statistics, September 1990):1.

16. The Earthworks Group, *Fifty Simple Things You Can Do to Save the Earth* (Berkeley, Calif.: Earthworks Press, 1989), p. 52.

17. King, *Strength to Love*, p. 31.

18. Lecture (August 1975), Summertown, Tennessee.

GLOSSARY

altruism: doing good for others without expecting a reward

amoral: when a situation is neither moral nor immoral

character: the overall combination of a person's moral traits

conscience: what you have already learned about right and wrong; the knowledge you use to make your moral decisions

divine revelation: what is revealed by God

empathy: connecting emotionally with other people; feeling as they feel

ethics: the study of morality; learning about right and wrong, and good and bad

guilt: feeling remorse for something done

immoral: in ethics, wrong or bad behavior

intolerance: disrespect for a different viewpoint or behavior

moral: in ethics, what is good or right

moral agency and moral autonomy: having the ability to make your own moral decisions

moral ambiguity: confusion or uncertainty about what is moral or immoral in a particular situation

moral awareness: realizing that a situation is morally right or wrong, and that certain situations have ethical considerations

moral compass: the moral principles and values you use to determine how you want to live morally

moral conflict: when you know what is right but struggle over whether or not to do it

moral culpability: responsibility for what you have done wrong

moral good: what is of value in moral living

personal ethics: ethics that have to do with our character and with ourselves and our relations to others

retribution: making up or paying back for a mistake or wrongdoing

self-righteous: believing your viewpoint is the only right one, and refusing to be open-minded about any other opinions

tolerance: being fair toward others who are different from you, and being open-minded about moral viewpoints that are different from your own

virtue: moral excellence, such as courage, wisdom, and kindness

SELECTED BIBLIOGRAPHY

Books

Black, Algernon. *The First Book of Ethics*. New York: Franklin Watts, 1965.

Browne, Ray, ed. *Contemporary Heroes and Heroines*. New York: Gale Research, 1990.

Coles, Robert. *The Moral Life of Children*. Boston: Houghton Mifflin, 1986.

———. *The Spiritual Life of Children*. Boston: Houghton Mifflin, 1990.

Damon, William. *The Moral Child*. New York: Free Press, 1989.

Frankl, Viktor E. *Man's Search for Meaning*. New York: Washington Square Press, 1984.

Franklin, Benjamin. *Poor Richard's Almanack*. reprinted. Mount Vernon, N.Y.: Peter Pauper Press.

Gilligan, Carol. *In a Different Voice*. Cambridge, Mass.: Harvard University Press, 1982.

Hersh, Seymour M. *Cover-up*. New York: Random House, 1972.

Hunt, Morton. *The Compassionate Beast*. New York: William Morrow, 1990.

Kohlberg, Lawrence. *The Philosophy of Moral Development*. Vol. 1. San Francisco: Harper & Row, Publ., 1981.

Milgram, Stanley. *Obedience to Authority*. New York: Harper & Row, Publ., 1974.

Newton, Lisa H. *Ethics in America: Source Reader.* Englewood Cliffs, N.J.: Prentice Hall, 1989.

_____. *Ethics in America: Study Guide.* Englewood Cliffs, N.J.: Prentice Hall, 1989.

Oliner, Samuel P., and Oliner, Pearl. *The Altruistic Personality: Rescuers of Jews in Nazi Europe.* New York: Free Press, 1988.

Radest, Howard. *Can We Teach Ethics?* New York: Praeger, 1989.

Scheleff, Leon. *The Bystander.* Lexington, Mass.: Lexington Books, 1978.

Schulman, Michael, and Mekler, Eva. *Bringing Up a Moral Child.* New York: Addison-Wesley, 1985.

Stein, Harry. *Ethics (and Other Liabilities).* New York: St. Martin's Press, 1982.

Yee, Min S., and Layton, Thomas N., *In My Father's House: The Story of the Layton Family and the Reverend Jim Jones.* New York: Holt, Rinehart and Winston, 1981.

Articles and Pamphlets

Bodian, Stephan. "Love Is the Healer: An Interview with Joan Borysenko." *Yoga Journal,* May/June 1990, pp. 44–9.

Bowen, Ezra. "What Ever Became of Honest Abe?" *Time,* April 4, 1988, p. 68.

Chira, Susan. "Princeton Student's Brainstorm: A Peace Corps To Train Teachers." *New York Times,* June 20, 1990.

Coles, Robert, and Genevie, Louis, eds. *The Girl Scout Survey on the Beliefs and Moral Values of America's*

Children. New York: Girl Scouts of America, Fall 1989.

"The Ferrell Family's Unlikely Crusade." *McCall's,* January 1985, p. 54.

Foderaro, Lisa. "At Rye High, Students Not Only Must Do Well, They Must Do Good." *New York Times,* April 30, 1990.

Goldman, Daniel. "Studies on Development of Empathy Challenge Some Old Assumptions." *New York Times,* July 12, 1990.

Hall, Trish. "How Classroom Crusaders Saved the Dolphin from the Net." *New York Times,* April 18, 1990.

Hueber, Graham. "Pharmacists and Clergy Again Rated Highest for Honesty and Ethical Standards." Gallup Poll News Service, February 28, 1990.

Robbins, William. "Acts of Charity Spring from Rock of Honesty." *New York Times,* December 16, 1990.

Steinem, Gloria. "If Moral Decay Is the Question, Is a Feminist Ethic the Answer?" *Ms.,* September 1987, pp. 57–64.

Steinfels, Peter. "Beliefs: Survey of Students Yields Some Insights on How They Reach Decisions on Moral Issues." *New York Times,* March 17, 1990.

Teltsch, Kathleen. "Couple Hunts Rare Animal: American Giraffe." *New York Times,* March 7, 1988.

INDEX

ABOUT THE AUTHOR

SUSAN NEIBURG TERKEL is the author of several well-received books for young people, including *Abortion: Facing the Issues*, *Understanding Child Custody*, and *Should Drugs Be Legalized?* She holds a degree in Child Development and Family Relationships from Cornell University.

Ms. Terkel lives in Ohio with her husband, Larry, and their children, Ari, Marni, and David.